Opening Tricks

OPENING TRICKS

EDITED BY PETER CARVER

THISTLEDOWN PRESS LTD.

Foreword: Peter Carver

Canadian Cataloguing in Publication Data

Main entry under title:
Opening tricks

An anthology of humourous short fiction for young adult readers, selected from Thistledown's third cross-Canada competition.
ISBN 1-895449-78-2

1. Short stories, Canadian (English).* 2. Canadian wit and humor (English).* 3. Young adult fiction, Canadian (English).* 4. Canadian fiction (English) — 20th century.* I. Carver, Peter, 1936- II. Thistledown Press Ltd.

PS8323.H85 O64 1998 C813'.01089283 C98-920172-4
PR9197.35.H85 O64 1998

Cover design by A.M. Forrie
Typeset by Thistledown Press Ltd.

Printed and bound in Canada by
Veilleux Impression à Demande
Boucherville, Quebec

Thistledown Press Ltd.
633 Main Street
Saskatoon, Saskatchewan
S7H 0J8

Thistledown Press gratefully acknowledges the financial assistance of the Canada Council for the Arts, the Saskatchewan Arts Board, and the Government of Canada through the Book Publishing Industry Development Program for its publishing program.

Publisher's Message

Thistledown Press continues to publish anthologies that offer audiences the most diversified and well-written work that we can find. This tradition continues with *Opening Tricks*, a lively, contemporary, humourous collection of fiction edited by Peter Carver.

Theresa Ford observed in her introduction to *Canadian Humour and Satire*: "Humour is a facet of our personalities that varies tremendously from person to person." Still, all readers know when writers achieve a humourous moment: the fractured logic, the character incongruity, the blatent irony. *Opening Tricks* endeavours to make those reader connections. Its stories are clearly set to divert us from weighty explorations of the human condition that inspect and dissect our serious natures. Those diversions are here.

Without taking our humour too seriously, we have found stories that searched out the hidden absurdities, the logical contradictions and pulled from the grab bag of farce, nonsense, dilemma, whimsey and tall-tales the energy that makes sometimes unique, other times familiar commentaries on contemporary lives. Though readers will no doubt discover the stylistic differences of the stories, they will also discover the shared vision and the common aim — to make someone laugh.

Contents

FOREWORD

Stephen Leacock, one of Canada's lesser known political economists and perhaps our greatest humourist, once wrote: "Humour is essentially a comforter, reconciling us to things as they are in contrast to things as they might be." In the work of the best humourists, there is a sad streak, a perception that life is not perfect and that as human beings we tend to fall short. We laugh at our shortcomings, but there's a dark side to that laugh as well.

The third Thistledown YA fiction contest is informed by this elusive comic muse. Funnily enough, humour is difficult to write — humour that engages, entertains, and somehow or another makes you laugh. One reason is that much of the humour we enjoy has that "you had to be there" quality; it's private, a matter of taste. Nobody else gets it.

In this group of stories we hope that there are no private jokes, that the various sources of humour are accessible to all.

For example, in the rueful awareness that, even in the midst of mourning, there is a kind of absurd urge to recapture what is lost that makes us do crazy things, attach our hopes to impossible circumstances — and then perhaps find some sort of peace.

Or, in a charmed moment wherein a young man, uncertain of himself, finds assurance and courage to deal with the hostile forces in his life; we laugh at his triumph because it is so unlikely but yet completely credible — particularly because it draws from one of the classic expressions of trickery in our lore.

There's the rueful humour which accompanies young people's early attempts to form relationships, profound or not. Even in the steamy throes of romance, the mis-fires and mis-matings have about them a kind of comic flamboyance at which we can all shake our heads and breathe a smile of recognition.

Young people love to shock and outrage each other and the world, and the comic spirit of "gross-out" can be found here. And the predicaments kids get into, sometimes by trying to keep up an image, are always worth chuckles.

Another target of humour is that tricky transition from adolescence to adulthood, those months and years when we try to demonstrate wit and understanding beyond our years, to paste on an expression of worldly knowledge that we don't really possess — and maybe never will.

Then there's the sheerly delightful whimsy of the fanciful, whether it's found in the contemporary world or in a time long past.

Finally we're reminded that one of the richest and most complex sources of humour lies in our recognition of human imperfections, a recognition that is coupled with compassion and understanding.

Comic relief? Yes, in the truest sense. Enjoy these worlds.

The Trickster

Jacqueline Pearce

Josh eased into the last empty seat on the bus, trying not to jostle the cardboard box he carried. The top flaps wouldn't close properly, and he was afraid the smell might leak out. With the box in his arms, he couldn't take his backpack off and lean back. He felt crowded and conspicuous. He wished he hadn't agreed to go to the university to pick the stuff up for his mom. Lately, he hated going anywhere on the bus or Skytrain — since those guys had jumped him to steal his leather jacket. The last thing he wanted to do was draw attention to himself. What if someone asked him about the box? He imagined the conversation.

"What's in the box?"

"A dead coyote."

"Huh?"

"I'm serious. A deceased . . . " What had that woman at the university called it? *Canis latrans.* You know, Latin for "barking dog".

♣♣♣

Josh thought back to the meeting at the university. His mom had needed the coyote skull and pelt for a project she was doing with her grade six class. She couldn't get to the university before the Department of Animal Science resource centre closed, so she'd persuaded Josh to go for her. By the time the bus rolled onto the university campus, he was wondering if she might have had an ulterior motive. Like, maybe she figured he needed a push to get out doing things on transit again. He almost turned to leave right then.

Finding the resource centre in the corridors of the science building was like trying to find a tiny piece of cheese in a maze. (Rats, mice, cats, roadrunners . . . that's what coyotes ate, wasn't it?) The room Josh finally entered was lined floor to ceiling with books. One wall was covered with shelves of stuffed dead animals. A raccoon. An owl. Lots of smaller birds. At the back of the room, a young woman was bent over a desk, writing.

"Excuse me. I'm here to pick up some coyote stuff."

"Oh, hi. Right. Just a minute." She stood up and disappeared into a back room. Whoa, she was good looking. Okay, she was at least five years older than he was, but that could work, couldn't it? Maybe this wouldn't be a wasted afternoon after all. Josh wondered if he could pass for a university student. What had he said when he came in? Had he already blown it? Try and sound older, smarter. What was some of that stuff Mom had been babbling about coyotes? They were related to wolves, foxes, even dogs. They hunted in packs, usually — except when they lived in the city. Yeah, that's right. City coyotes usually lived alone — or with a mate. He liked the sound of that last word.

For a minute, Josh imagined a coyote, long-legged, yellow-brown, wandering along the edge of an alley. A predator on the prowl. The young woman came back into the room. Josh stopped slouching, stood as tall as possible.

"Here you go. One *Canis latrans*," she said, setting down a bundle of yellow-brown fur on the counter, along with a white skull that looked the shape of a dog's head. It was just fur and bones, but it still had an animal smell to it.

"What?" Josh asked, stupidly.

"It's the Latin name," she explained. "It means 'barking dog'."

"Oh, right."

Something small, grey-white, and pointed rolled across the counter. She picked it up.

"Oh, if any of the teeth fall out, just stick them back in."

She folded the skull and pelt together and wrapped them with tissue paper and something that looked like couch stuffing. Then she bent down behind the counter and came back up with the box.

Josh cleared his throat. Okay, maybe he'd had a bad start, but things were still salvageable. *Say something, you idiot.*

"Ah, so do you get a lot of demand for dead coyotes?" *Oh, that was brilliant.*

She smiled, carefully stuffing the bundle into the box.

"Not exactly," she said. "Though a lot of people seem to prefer them dead to alive."

He could tell by the way she said this that she was not one of those people. He remembered something his mom had said about people in the past trying to wipe out coyotes. Also, about some people now not being too happy to have coyotes around the city.

"I guess they have a bit of a PR problem," he said, aiming for what he hoped was a kind of intellectual humour.

"You could say that." She seemed to appreciate his comment. "It's true they have lowered the city cat population a bit. But they've lowered the rat population a lot more."

"Right," Josh nodded. He was finding the topic much more interesting now than he had when his mom had tried to talk to him about coyotes.

"It's ironic," she went on. "Coyotes are one of the few wild animals that have expanded their numbers and territory — despite people trying to get rid of them."

"Really?" He wanted her to keep talking, so he could keep looking at her.

"Yeah. It's because they're so good at adapting to things. That's why they can move into the city and do so well."

"Plus, they're not picky eaters," Josh put in. She laughed.

Josh was beginning to feel that maybe things were going all right between them, after all. Adaptable, he thought. That's me. Fitting in with university students wasn't so tough. She handed him the box, still smiling. She had a great smile. He pictured the hunting coyote, senses alert, ready to pounce. This was it.

"Do you want to go for a coffee?" he asked her straight out.

"I'd love to."

Okay, so that last bit was how he rewrote the conversation afterward, sitting on the bus. In actual fact, he'd taken the box from her and sputtered something like, "See you around." As he'd left, he imagined the coyote again. Ahead of the coyote, a rat ran down the alley and scuttled under a fence. Once out of the building, Josh realized he'd been wearing his Fraser High School jacket the whole time. What an idiot.

♣♣♣

Josh squirmed mentally in the bus seat. Of course he was wearing the dumb high school jacket instead of his leather one. Even when he managed to put getting mugged the other night out of his mind, it still came back to stalk him. Now, the whole scene began replaying in his mind again. He'd been on his way to Nick's house around nine o'clock, got off at the Skytrain stop, and there they were. Four guys about his age, leaning against the railing by the steps to the street.

"Hey, nice jacket," one of the guys said. He had a dark narrow face and wore a blue bandanna tied around the top of his head. Two other guys stepped toward him.

"Why don't you give us your jacket?"

At first Josh thought maybe they were joking. He laughed. Okay, well, he tried to laugh. It sounded more like a squeaky door imitation.

"You laughing at us?" All four pressed in on him. There was something tight and coiled up about them. As if they could let go and do anything. Josh glanced around. The Skytrain stop and the surrounding street looked deserted.

The guy with the bandanna shoved him. He fell against a big guy who felt kind of soft. Like the Pilsbury Dough Boy, Josh thought briefly, stupidly. Dough Boy grabbed Josh by the collar.

"You looking for a fight?"

Okay, they wanted an excuse to let go on him.

"Just a minute." Josh took off his leather jacket — not to give it to them, just to free up his arms. He dropped the coat to the ground and sprung into Kung Fu readiness.

Okay, so that's where the replay deviated a bit from what actually happened that night. In actual fact, he'd dropped the jacket and run.

On the bus, Josh wondered what the woman at the university would have thought of him if she'd known what happened that night — how shaken up he'd been. He still felt unnerved, off balance. He couldn't even go out of the house without looking over his shoulder. He felt uncomfortable around people in a way he hadn't before. All because of some jerks. His stomach twisted with frustration and anger. Part of him wished he could have fought them and hurt them. He felt like a coward for giving up his jacket so easily and running. But then, on the other hand, running was not so stupid. He was still in one piece, wasn't he? So what if he lost an expensive piece of clothing? He'd done what he needed to survive — like the coyote.

Josh tried to concentrate his thoughts on the woman in the biology museum and forget about the other stuff. It was a much better memory — even if he didn't adjust it here and there. Maybe she had known he was in high school, but he'd still had a good conversation with her. She'd even laughed at his jokes. So what if he hadn't asked her out? So what if he hadn't even asked her name? The fact was, he'd had a good conversation with a great-looking older woman who hadn't even cared that he was younger. Maybe he could feel good about the whole thing after all.

As he looked out the bus window, something caught Josh's eye, and he shifted his focus from inside his head to outside the window. Had he seen a flash of yellow-brown tail, as some animal trotted around the back corner of a 7-Eleven store? He shifted the box on his lap, remembering the dead coyote. Had that coyote lived around here when it was alive? It was hard to imagine such a large wild animal living in the city. They were smart, elusive — tricky, even. He might have walked right by a coyote's hiding place and never known. He'd certainly never seen one — at least not that he knew of. He smiled to himself, remembering how coyotes in legends could change shape from one thing to another. Coyote shape one minute, human shape the next. Sometimes the legend Coyote gave things to people, sometimes he tricked them out of things. You never knew what to expect. Pretty cool, really.

Josh looked up. There was a bad smell on the bus. People were wrinkling their noses and glancing around. It smelled close — like some loser with really bad BO had sat right behind him. Man, it was bad — almost like a dead animal. Oh. Josh stared at the box on his lap. The flaps were wide open. Quickly, he closed it back up, hoping no one had noticed. The bus came to a stop and several people got out.

"That's better," a woman a couple of seats up remarked when the door had closed behind the last person. She was looking out the window at the departing backs, shaking her head. Josh let out a sigh of relief.

At the front of the bus, a noisy group of girls was getting on. They were maybe a bit younger than Josh. Probably coming from some after-school practice, he guessed. He knew this stop was near Livingston, a rival high school to his. Across the street from the bus, Josh could see a bunch of kids spilling out of a pizza/video game place. Three guys were leaning against a shiny black Mazda parked in front. Suddenly, with a sick feeling, Josh recognized them. One wore a blue bandanna just like the other night. Dough Boy was there and one of the others. That one was wearing a leather jacket just like the one Josh had lost. Josh's first instinct was to duck, melt into the seat. His heart pounded.

Cautiously, he looked again. There was the fourth guy a few feet from the car, talking to a girl with long brown hair. She was holding onto his arm as if she wanted to keep him with her, but he was shaking his head and pulling away. The other three guys got into the car. The fourth guy tried to kiss the girl, but she didn't seem to want to kiss him back. He hesitated, then shrugged and turned to join the others. The bus started to move then. Josh could still see the girl standing on the sidewalk, arms crossed, watching the black car pull away. She didn't look happy.

Josh turned away from the window. He realized he was sweating. He'd been afraid of seeing them again, and now he had — he'd seen them, and nothing had happened. It was weird how ordinary they seemed. It almost gave him a feeling of power to know that he'd watched part of their lives — perhaps even knew something about them — and they hadn't even seen him.

A screech of tires drew Josh's attention to the window again. The black car had made a U-turn and was now picking up speed and passing the bus. Josh could hear the booming bass of the car stereo as it passed right under his window. He wondered where they were going, what they were planning to do.

It was almost dark out now, and the bus's progress was painfully slow. It seemed to be stopping at every stop and at every light. Finally, the bus pulled up next to the

Skytrain station where Josh got off. From here, he could transfer to another bus for a five-minute trip home or walk the rest of away. Several people passed him, heading for the steps to the Skytrain. Josh checked his watch. It was a twenty-minute wait until the next bus. Might as well walk. Josh hesitated, then stepped out of the lighted area onto the dark sidewalk.

It was then that he saw them. They were leaning on the black Mazda, parked where they could watch people come and go from the Skytrain and buses. Josh's heart jumped, and his hands on the box grew immediately sweaty. What were they doing here? Had they followed him? No, they couldn't have. Cruising Skytrain stops was their thing, wasn't it? Seeing them now was just a coincidence, right? They were just here waiting for some poor victim to walk off into the dark alone — like he'd just done. Well, they hadn't noticed him yet. He could turn around and go back to the lit station. And then what? Cower there until they drove off? No, keep going. Maybe he could get around the corner before they even noticed him. Too late. They were coming.

Josh kept walking, forcing himself to stay calm. Maybe they wouldn't bother him. Maybe they were just going somewhere in this direction. Maybe cows could fly. Who was he kidding?

"Hey, wait a minute," one of them called in a deceptively friendly voice. They jogged a bit to catch up to him.

Images flashed in his mind. The coyote, the rat, himself holding the box, the coyote again — one image transforming into another.

"What's in the box?" The guy with the bandanna had come up on one side of Josh, Dough Boy on the other. They pressed closer. This can't be happening again. It was like in the nightmares he'd been having. Someone shoved him from behind.

"Are you deaf? We asked you, what's in the box?" Josh turned to look at the guy who'd spoken. It was the one with the girlfriend. Josh remembered how he'd looked on the street with her — pleading, apologetic. Now, he was changed — swaggering, confident. The others, too, had an edge to them that hadn't been there when he watched them unobserved from the bus window. They'd seemed like ordinary individual guys then. Now they were something else — tied together, fuelling each other. They moved closer, like one body, pressing him on all sides.

Josh felt like a cornered animal — panicked, frozen. He thought of the fragile skull being pulled out, laughed at, smashed on the ground. The pelt being stepped on. He thought of himself running again — running and running, always looking over his shoulder. Anger flared in his gut, then was gone. He realized he no longer felt afraid. Instead, he felt sort of numb and strangely detached.

Hands grabbed for the box. Josh felt a small click inside himself — like something moved, shifted, and snapped into a new place. With one easy movement, he opened the box flaps and reached his right hand inside. Carefully, he placed his fingers on the furred nose of the pelt head and the skull beneath it. For a moment, the bodies around him drew back, giving space. Swiftly Josh drew out his hand, gripping fur and bone. He thrust the grinning coyote head in Dough Boy's face and growled. It was a deep, menacing animal sound — not human at all.

"Huh?" Dough Boy stepped back, surprised. Josh almost jumped back in surprise, himself. But before he had a chance to think about what he was doing, he jerked around and lunged the skull at the next guy.

"I am Coyote," a gravelly voice rose out of the dark, authoritative and mocking. It finished the statement with a sharp yipping howl. What the . . . ? Had he actually just howled?

"I have other names, too," the voice continued. "You don't know me, but I know you. I know everything about you — where you live, what school you go to . . . " Josh sensed a movement behind him and whipped around.

"Livingston High School," the coyote voice hissed. Josh heard several sharp intakes of breath. Someone swore. Dough Boy laughed, but it sounded nervous, uncertain. Josh wondered why they didn't do something — didn't try to shut him up. This whole thing was crazy. He was crazy.

The pelt moved again, the tips of the hairs shining for a moment in the dark. Josh felt himself take two steps. They were no longer pressing in on him.

"I know a brown-haired girl who wants you to play," the coyote teeth flashed in front of the fourth guy. "You keep leaving her, you're going to lose her . . . "

"Hey, how does he — ?"

Josh turned again, facing the guy with the leather jacket. The guy glanced toward the car, as if he'd rather be getting in it than standing so close to Josh.

"You shouldn't wear things that aren't yours," the coyote voice chided. "Someone might not like it."

"Geez . . . " The guy looked around, as if for some direction, but none of the others met his eyes.

"Come on." The guy with the bandanna punched Dough Boy on the arm. His voice sounded deflated. "Let's go . . . this guy's nuts."

"Yeah, this is getting boring." The guy with the leather jacket turned away, started walking in the direction of the waiting car. Josh could hardly believe this was happening. They were actually walking away — leaving him.

The coyote pelt continued to jerk and move, the voice yipping softly, as the four guys climbed into the black car. The engine revved, and the car pulled away from the curb with a squeal.

Standing alone on the sidewalk, Josh dropped his arm and let out a long breath. He bent down to set the cardboard box on the sidewalk, so he could fold the coyote pelt back inside. His knees felt suddenly weak, and his hands were shaking. He looked at the pale skull in his hands. A moment before, it had seemed so full of power — so alive. He shook his head. What had just happened, exactly?

Something small and whitish tinked onto the sidewalk and rolled in a short arc. A tooth. Josh laughed, feeling close to normal again. He picked up the tooth and placed it back in the coyote jaw. Then he packed the skull and pelt back in the box, closed the flaps, and stood up. Ahead of him the street was dark, but he didn't mind. He began walking, feeling a prickle of elation rise up his neck. What the hell. He tilted his head back and howled — a laughing, yowling animal-human sound.

"Mom?!"

Diana C. Aspin

"Dalai, Lama, rama, rama," Ruby Tackaberry sang. For as far as she was concerned it was already a done deal; this beautiful, brown-eyed boy in her tender care *was* the reincarnation of her dead mother.

"Dalai, Lama, rama, rama," Ruby chanted with each click of the kid's stroller wheels across the sidewalk. A shoulder bag full of blankets, toy cars, and diapers pulsed against her hip, and little green buds like Hershey's Kisses sprouted from the black limbs of trees. Ruby felt like a kiss herself, light and promising, not as she'd felt for the past nine months, heavy and hollow, her heart as unyielding as a clenched fist. All that remained, when she got Jamile Rohan Siddiqui to her house, was to confirm his identity.

Jamile leaned back suddenly, pointed up, and gurgled. Above them a crow glided against a backdrop of cerulean sky, the sun glinting blackish-purple off its wings, a mess of nesting material dangling from its beak.

"Test time, Kiddo," Ruby said, leaning over and planting a kiss on his nose.

♣♣♣

It all began with the East Indian dreams. Ruby had crawled into her parents' bed the day she had the rim of her right ear tattooed with her mom's name, Pearl. Piteously, she'd nosed about in the frilly pillow for some vestige of her mom: a smudge of Tangerine Jamboree lipstick, a trace of rose perfume, a filament of hair — and, coming up empty, she'd sobbed herself to sleep.

She'd woken with a crashing headache and a memory of three ultra-vivid dreams.

Dreams which would change everything.

In one, she and her mom sopped up the juices of a goat curry with nan bread. In another, her mom line danced down the aisles of an Indian carpet emporium, the front panels of her embroidered, denim vest opening and closing like a pair of doors. In the most bizarre dream, Ruby pushed an Indian baby boy around in a stroller and she leaned down and kissed his cheek and called him 'Mom'.

Mom?!

At school, in the shadow of the bleachers, Ruby watched her best friend, Destiny, gorge herself on a mess of sprouts and beans and told her about the dreams.

"Wow," Destiny said, her blue eyes wide behind her steel-framed glasses. "Synchronicity."

Ruby thought it sounded New Age and suspect. Destiny's mom, Poppy, messed about with Tarot cards and the *I Ching* and ate only "organic".

"A meaningful coincidence," Destiny explained. "A happy accident. Like when you've been thinking of someone for days and — bingo! — they knock on your door. Or like your dreams." Destiny licked her finger and culled sprout heads from her long, flowered skirt. "Listen up, Ruby. The universe is speaking to you."

"Stuff the universe," Ruby said. She'd rather her *mom* spoke to her than have the universe drop in for a meaningful chat.

Destiny shivered and ducked out into the sunlight.

"That's the problem with you, Ruby, you're so closed-minded." She snatched up her hemp lunch bag and marched off.

"Okay then, Miss Know-It-All!" Ruby shouted after her. "What *do* my dreams mean?"

"What else?" Destiny said, twirling about. "Why *Indian* food? Why *Indian* rugs? Your mom's out there somewhere, reincarnated, starting over."

Wow. The thought of her mom guzzling at some dark breast, developing a taste for off-key music and goat curry, made Ruby's scalp shift, as though her skull was the earth itself, its plates easing together to make brand new continents.

That night Ruby grabbed the newspaper containing her mom's death announcement and sussed out the birth column. Almost fainted for — yes! — Jamile Rohan had been born to Zaheda and Shafeeq Siddiqui the very night her mom died. And perhaps the universe *was* speaking to her because the Siddiquis lived only a block away. All she had to do was offer to babysit.

Dad won't swing for it, she thought, but she needed to tell him.

♣♣♣

"Dad?" Ruby whispered, slipping into the living room.

Back and forth, back and forth across bare boards tall, skinny Rod Tackaberry of Tackaberry's Auto Service line danced to some achey breaky hurtin' tune. The light winked off the silver spurs of his brown western boots, flashed off his silver and turquoise belt buckle, sparked off the silvery balls at the end of his tasselled vest. All on his owny-O, his arm around her dead mom's waist, his face shaded by the wide brim of his cowboy hat. On the green checkered sofa, from the shocked mouth of her mom's purse, spilled a jumbled conversation of lipsticks, pizza coupons, and her favourite Day-Glo bingo markers. Her dad was in a time warp. Big time.

Ruby sat down heavily on the carpet her dad had rolled up to make way for a dance floor after her mom died. He smiled down at the sofa, then stepped back into a swarm of dust bunnies the size of tumbleweed to let Ruby's mom glide by.

One cylinder short of an engine, Ruby thought. People did weird things when their hearts were broken, didn't they? Look at what she'd done to herself: the rim of her right ear tattooed with her mom's name, the rim of the other stuck with eight silver rings, her hair worried into an angry pincushion of blue spikes.

When her friend Emma's grandfather died, his wife, who'd been a butcher in Hungary before the revolution, shut herself in the garage for three days. Singing and sobbing, "*Sandor, szeretlek, Sandor, szeretlek,*" she oh-so-tenderly sawed the head off a whole pig and ladled the rest of the hacked-up corpse into freezer bags. Ruby prayed, as her dad bowed politely to the coffee table, that there was a time limit on grieving.

When the music stopped, her dad sat next to her on the rolled-up carpet and positioned his hat between what she called, when she was little, his pointy-ointy boots. "What's going down, Rube?"

"I had these weird dreams, Dad."

"Aha."

The bare boards were icy cold and Ruby drew her feet up and tucked them inside her pyjama legs. "Destiny seems to think that Mom's been, well, reincarnated."

Her dad took in her angry spikes, her messed up ears, her new black lipstick — Gothic Dread. He had the dark, desperate look of a coal miner stuck in the wrong tunnel, frantic for a sliver of light. "Come again?"

"I hate to tell you this, Dad, but we think Mom's started over."

"Let me get this straight," he said, lifting his hat and pressing his forehead into its wide brim, "you think Pearl's back. Like, on this planet?"

"Weird but true." Ruby shrugged deeper into her pyjamas.

"Look, Rube, don't you think it's about time we got on with our lives? Like . . . like I could roll back this carpet and take the old Corvette for a spin and you could —"

"Hold it, Dad! There's more."

"More?" Dark circles, like petals, bloomed under his shocked eyes.

"Yes, I've found Mom. And I'm going to see if her . . . well, *his*, parents need a babysitter."

"You've got to be joking!"

"No, I'm not." Ruby spoke to the penguins on the knees of her pyjamas. "Mom is now Jamile Rohan Siddiqui."

"You've *got* to be joking!"

"I know it sounds nuts but I have this gut feeling."

"So do I, Rube! And it's not pleasant. I should never have bought you that damned Ouija board."

"Ouija?" Ruby said, leaning forward, smiling. "Dad! You remember that?"

"Remember it! You and Destiny Ouija'd up Lizzie Borden!"

Ruby remembered too. She'd heard Lizzie Borden's stiff skirt skimming the floor, the swish of her axe, her hot, murderous breath. Her mom slept with her that night and Ruby had wound her fingers so tight around her mom's nightie straps that no one, not even Lizzie Borden, could have extricated her.

"These dreams were so real, Dad. Different than normal dreams."

"Oh, Rube," her dad groaned, and when he'd trudged off Ruby shampooed the blue from her hair, whipped out her earrings, and scrubbed her face squeaky, babysitter clean. In the bathroom mirror she practised a Brady Bunch smile and said, "Ooochy, coochy, coo."

♣♣♣

Zaheda, in blue jeans and a yellow and gold tunic top, had a clipped way of talking, her words rising and falling on the spice-scented air like nervous little birds. She invited Ruby inside to meet Jamile. "I planned to place an ad for a sitter today. What a coincidence."

In the middle of the kitchen floor a tiny boy sat, clutching a blue blanket, his first finger hooked securely into the corner of his mouth.

Mom? Ruby thought, as Jamile crawled over to his mother, his fat, diapered bum gyrating from side to side. Could it really be her mom? That bronzed skin, those huge brown eyes? She resisted the urge to scoop him up and whack the breath out of him with a hug. When he turned around, Ruby flashed him a smile fit to blind him, followed by a knowing wink.

Zaheda handed Jamile a yellow, lidded mug of milk and rolled a model car in his direction. "Jamile is crazy about cars," she laughed.

But what, Ruby thought, about wild lipsticks and bingo and dancing the night away to hurtin' tunes? How to know if little blanket-man here was her mom?

While Zaheda brewed jasmine tea, Ruby dropped to her haunches and held out her hands to the boy. He shuffled over, curious.

Mom, she mouthed at him. *It's me, Ruby. Give me a sign.*

Jamile hauled a handful of blanket to his mouth and began to suck noisily at it, his bottom lip trembling.

Ruby flushed with shame. I'm a psychopath, she thought. Yet, if Jamile *was* her mom . . .

Over the following weeks, in vain, Ruby searched for signs while she babysat at Jamile's house. Then it was arranged she babysit one Saturday, for the whole day. And yes, Zaheda said, Ruby could take him to meet her dad and Destiny.

♣♣♣

Ruby was in the supermarket, absorbed in thought about the upcoming meeting, wondering how she could determine that Jamile *was* her mom, when she rolled her cart smack into the knees of a guy with a shaved head. Such kind, brown eyes, and a laugh which rose up like a wave from his belly, loud and deep.

And along with the wave of laughter, miraculously, the answer to her problem.

The guy was the image of a Tibetan monk in a film she'd seen with Destiny a few months ago. The monk had been searching for the reincarnation of Tibet's religious head honcho, the Dalai Lama. Ruby remembered how a little boy reached for some beads which had belonged to the previous holy man and said: "Mine!"

To be absolutely certain the boy was the Dalai Lama, the monks had shown him a selection of eyeglasses, fancy prayer rattles and whatnot. And each time — bingo! —

he picked the ones which had belonged to the dead Dalai Lama.

That was it! With her mother's stuff, say her bingo marker and favourite lipstick, Ruby would test Jamile Rohan Siddiqui.

She shared her plan with her dad. He was hovering over the messy kitchen counter, his hands and face blotched with engine grease, biting into a cheese and tomato sandwich. "I don't think you should mess with this stuff, Rube. It's dangerous."

"Dad! It's not an exorcism. Mom's not going to rush down the stairs in a river of ectoplasm."

"Rube! Your mom is *not* an Indian baby. Your mom is . . . " his voice cracked, "dead."

Ruby said, "Dad, I have to."

He tossed the rest of his sandwich into the garbage and closed the door with the heel of his work boot. "Rube, every morning I wake up and I don't believe this is happening to me."

"Me too, Dad." They were silent then, really looking at each other for the first time since her mom died. There were tomato seeds between his teeth and a crumb of bread stuck to his cheek which her mom would have reached out, laughing, and picked off. The clenched fist in Ruby's chest opened in the silence.

♣♣♣

"Dalai, Lama, rama, rama." Ruby hauled Jamile from his stroller and hotfooted it into her house.

Her dad waited on the rolled-up carpet, head down, his face shaded by the brim of his hat. Destiny, who had helped Ruby organize the tests with the bingo marker and the lipsticks, sat beside him.

"Meet Rod," Ruby said, sitting next to her dad. Jamile clung to her and she could smell the baby powder in the folds of his neck and the sweet milk on his breath.

"Hi, little guy," Rod said with all the enthusiasm of a grease rag. He reached out and chucked him under the chin. Ruby noticed that her dad's huge hands had been scrubbed and his nails filed for the occasion.

Jamile slipped off her knee and shuffled over to Destiny who offered him a soya-bran-raisin bar. He took it but dropped it when he saw the box.

The night before, Ruby had flung tentacles of light into the crawl space with her flashlight and her dad had materialized on his hands and knees dragging an old box of her toys. "My contribution to the fiasco," he coughed.

Jamile fished out a naked fashion doll and sat gumming away at its ankle.

"I never saw Pearl do that," her dad said solemnly.

"You didn't know her when she played with dolls, Mr. T.," Destiny said.

Rod acquiesced. "True."

Once Jamile seemed relaxed, Ruby carried him over to the coffee table where a pen, pencil, and yellow bingo marker were lined up like sacrificial implements.

"Choose one," she said to him, straightening his collar. Until now she had not entertained the possibility that Jamile might prefer writing to bingo, or black lipstick to tangerine.

Her dad and Destiny hunkered down with Ruby. Destiny closed her eyes as Jamile's hand hovered over the table. Ruby held hers, prayer-shaped, in her lap. Jamile glanced from her dad to Ruby to Destiny, beaming with all the attention.

"Go ahead, little guy," Ruby urged. "Choose one."

"Maman-ala-bla-bla," Jamile gurgled and grabbed the yellow marker. "Mamama."

"He said, 'Mine'," Ruby cried.

"Praise be the Lord," Destiny shouted, and her words echoed around the uncarpeted room.

"This has gone too far," Rod said.

"We're in too deep, Mr T.," Destiny said.

"This isn't the bloody X-Files, Destiny."

"No cursing, Mr T." Destiny nodded toward Jamile who was bingo-markering his knee cap with the distracted, goggle-eyed fervour of a gold prospector.

Ruby's heart quickened. He looked not unlike her mom on bingo night!

"One more test, Dad, please."

He agreed and Jamile's hand circled the uncapped lipsticks: Pearl's Tangerine Jamboree, Ruby's Gothic Dread and Destiny's Mystic Lilac.

Jamile knelt there gazing at, and through, the lipsticks, deep in concentration.

"Cool," Destiny said. "He's remembering."

"A past life trance," Ruby exclaimed.

"Rubbish," her dad snapped, "he's pooping his pants!"

"Mr T.!"

At that Jamile came to, grabbed the Tangerine Jamboree — bingo! — and began smearing it over his face. He licked his lips and held up the tube. "Manam-bla!" he gurgled, blowing spit bubbles.

"He said, 'Mine'," Destiny cried and fell onto her back, her arms spread like wings.

"For goodness sakes, pull yourself together, Destiny," Rod said, although his pale-of-late cheeks were flushed and his sad eyes now bright. "It's pure coincidence."

Ruby's heart thrilled. She hadn't seen this much life in him since Mr. Atkinson's Oldsmobile blew up at the shop.

Destiny jerked upright. "It's not a coincidence, Mr. T. It's the universe speaking to us."

"Pfft!" Rod said. "What a load of mumbo jumbo."

"Mam-lib-ubla!" Jamile laughed and dribbled down his chin.

He was obviously feeling at home now.

And who *knew* to what extent!

He snatched up the flung hat and plonked it on his head. He smiled up at Rod, his mouth an orange gash in his small face.

"He looks like the Lone Ranger in drag!" Rod exclaimed.

"You're a scream, Mr. T.," Destiny said.

Jamile agreed. "Maman-isam-blub."

Ruby laughed and admired the messy circles at the crown of the little boy's dark head, admired his long, thick eyelashes, his white-booted feet, and she felt as though she had known him forever, not just in one or two lifetimes. There seemed to be so much happening that she did not understand. She slipped her mom's favourite line dancing CD into the player.

Jamile began to nod his head from side to side and stamp his heels on the floor. "Mimi-mimi. Bla-blub."

Rod whisked the boy up and began to dance with him hugged to his chest, dust bunnies scattering in their wake.

"Best get that carpet tacked down again," he whispered into Jamile's ear. "You'll be walking soon and we can't have you falling down."

"Blaba-daba-imbla," Jamile crooned, playing with Rod's ear. He hummed away to himself and then fell asleep, dribbling, spittle blooming darkly across Rod's denim shirt front.

"What do you think, Destiny?" Ruby curled up beside her on the sofa. Destiny tore open her box of apple-beet juice and passed it to Ruby who took a swig.

"I think he's the neatest kid I ever met," Destiny said.

"No, do you think he's my mom?"

"Do you?"

"He could be."

"Could be what?" Ruby's dad asked, sitting down on the carpet with a sleepy Jamile.

"Mom," Ruby said.

"Could be."

Jamile grinned and walked his little fingers up her dad's face, like a blind man reading braille. "Malam-amam-blub."

First Date

Eric Nicol

The first thing you need to understand about Morton Pilsworth is that he knew nothing about girls. Zilch. Zero. A big, fat doughnut.

Morton's ignorance about girls was not due to lack of interest. No way. Morton viewed girls as a fascinating mystery that he would gladly give all his earthly possessions — including his stamp collection — to be able to solve.

This urge to research the opposite sex was sharpened by awareness that, at fifteen, he was not getting any younger. Other guys at school were relatively worldly though only in Grade 10, where they seemed content to stay, confident that they knew enough about girls to get straight As in the subject, should the curriculum ever include this basic science.

Those guys were cool. Morton knew that he was not only uncool but visibly warm in the presence of an attractive girl. That is, his personal thermostat went ape. He strongly suspected that he actually radiated heat waves, like a highway in hot summer. Why, why, why? He felt cursed by a fatal allergy to something he craved, the way some kids felt about eating peanuts.

Yet he had tried. To grasp girls, that is, mentally if not physically. He had listened when his Socials teacher waded into Sex Education, demonstrating intercourse with a banana. But she didn't explain how the banana was so dramatically affected by the sight of a pair of adorable grapefruit.

So Morton continued to see sex as a much more complicated subject than Shop. And much as he ached to improve what his teacher called "social skills", *his* skills, when a pretty girl smiled at him, consisted of his face's flaming red, his stammering, and his hands clasping as though they didn't trust one another.

Morton thought he knew one reason why he was socially inept. He had been given the wrong name. His mother called him "Morton" (her maiden name), his father called him "Mortie", while his sister and other kids at school called him "Mort" — which the class brain told him was Latin for "dead".

Because of his name, Mort believed that he bore a curse, like King Tut's tomb. His relations with women were mortally doomed, by the simple fact that his parents had failed to provide him with a name — "Max" or "Mike" or "Elvis" — that created the illusion of vitality.

However, Mort had spunk. He had a good talk with himself one night when he couldn't get to sleep because he had happened to watch — while the rest of the family were out — a rented video titled Showgirls. Something about that educational documentary stiffened his resolve to overcome his name, and go for the previously unthinkable: a date with a girl.

He knew exactly which girl.

Her name was Adele. Adele was tall, blonde, beautiful, and cool. Seriously cool. Adele walked like a supermodel. Kids made way for Adele, even in their school's corridor zoo. Adele smoked with the Grade 12s in The Pit, the clump of cedars just outside the school grounds. Mort didn't smoke anywhere. His hockey coach had told him that if he ever smelt tobacco on Mort's breath he would strangle him with his own jockstrap.

But he could still aspire to Adele. In English class he had read Browning's lines: " . . . a man's reach should exceed his grasp/Or what's a heaven for?" Mort applied that reach to Adele. Heaven, in snug jeans. What he actually grasped, though, was that he was too shy to make the move on her. He was totally unsure of his personal magnetism. Profoundly, he wished that girls would be more overt in their readiness to be dated. Especially by him.

Some girls were shameless in the way they dropped their books near Herc Brandon, the hunky quarterback of the school's football team, and then made an enterprise of bending over to pick them up. Herc had no need to fear rejection. He benefitted from the First Law of Social Dynamics: rejections by girls increases in inverse ratio to height under six feet. At five-eight (in skates) Mort had every reason to anticipate his being turned down like a sickbed.

This was reality. But Mort's hurtling hormones still drove him to fantasize a date with Adele. How this miracle would occur, without their being the only two survivors of a shipwreck that cast them up on a desert island, was unclear to him. All he knew for sure was that he would have to ask her for a date in some way that limited the volume of crowd laughter when he was rejected. By carrier pigeon, maybe. Or, more practically, Mort lingered after school in the driveway, fussing with his bike and trusting Fate to effect an encounter, when Adele came out to be picked up by her mother's Jag.

Fate failed to cooperate. Once or twice Mort thought Adele noticed him, spinning his wheels literally. But she gave no indication that she had picked up the vibes of pure adoration.

Yet Mort continued to contribute to his date fund — sedulously segregated from his allowance — which would be ample to cover the movie, popcorn (large), and bus fare both ways. He would, of course, let Adele choose the movie, happy to brave a Restricted classification by wearing thick socks and thinking tall.

Then, out of the blue, came The Call.

Mort would never forget the circumstances of that historic moment. His sister, Melody, had got to the ringing phone first, as usual, then turned, agape, to tell him:

"It's for you."

He took the horn. "Hello?"

"Hi, Morton. It's Adele Pike-Forsyth."

His knees liquefied. "Hi, Adele!" (Drop your voice, man, you're fluting.)

"It's sort of short notice, but I wonder if you'd like to go with me to the Valentine Dance."

"The Valentine Dance . . . ?" (That was tomorrow evening. You don't know how to dance. Mission Impossible, man! Hang up, hang up!)

"Sure, Adele! I'd love to take you to the dance. Thanks for asking me — "

"Good. You can pick me up at eight, okay? You know my address?"

Mort broke the pencil lead, writing down the address of paradise found. "I'll find it, Adele . . . " (In a blinding snowstorm, if need be.) "Thanks again — " She had hung up.

Mort had to sit down. All parts of his body were reporting total ecstatic confusion. His brain was still in denial. But the lower organs were accepting the incredible joyfully. His mother found him in this traumatized state.

"Are you all right, Morton?"

Mort forced his eyes to focus on his mom. It wasn't easy. "Pardon?"

"You look as though you'd seen a ghost." (A ghost in spike heels, maybe.)

"Adele Pike-Forsyth has asked me to take her to the school Valentine Dance tomorrow night." The words were coming out of his mouth, but his mind still questioned the source.

"A dance? I didn't know you could dance."

"I can't. But I'll learn. I need a crash course in dancing, Mom." He gazed at his mother as fondly as only a child can when in desperate need of the unreasonable.

"Don't look at *me*," said his mom cordially. "I'm under doctor's orders not to tax my back. Ask your sister."

Mort retired to his room to assess this referral. It took him just thirty seconds to junk it. Even if his older sister accepted the assignment, she would probably show him how to do some dance that had gone out of style. The waltz, or polka, or something.

Mort took the problem to his father, who was lounged before the holy rectangle watching the Rangers destroy the Canucks.

"Dad," he said, "could you show me how to dance with a girl — between periods?"

His father winced. "Why do you want to know?"

"I have a date. Tomorrow night."

" . . . With a girl?" His father was a stickler for background material.

"Yes. And I'll have to dance with her . . . " Mort was suddenly engulfed by the enormity of the task. "Maybe I should phone her back and tell her I'm sorry but I've died . . . "

"No, no!" His father hastily turned off the TV. "You can handle this, son, believe me. If you can skate, you can dance."

Mort couldn't remember Wayne Gretzky's making any moves that would qualify him for the tango, but he was eager to be convinced. "Really?"

"Believe it." His father got up, grinning. "Arthur Murray taught me dancing in a hurry."

"Pardon me?"

"Just an old saying we had, when I was learning. Now listen to me carefully. Dancing basically is just putting your arm around the girl's waist and shuffling your feet in time to the music." His father grabbed him around the middle. "Then your left hand takes hold of her right hand so that your partner can't hit you because of what your other hand is doing."

Mort bit a lip. "Are you sure people still dance that way?"

"No, I'm not. In my time the man was supposed to lead, but that may have changed."

"Lead where?"

"Around the floor. Don't lead her into areas that are not well lit. You could have an accident."

His father let go of him, but not before Melody had come into the room.

"Maybe you two would like to be alone," she smirked.

Mr. Pilsworth hastily lapsed back into his chair and sought sanctuary in the remote.

"Dad was showing me how to dance," Mort said. "I have a date."

"So I heard." Melody smiled like a lizard sizing up a fat gnat. "A date with a *girl*! Congratulations! Who's the lucky woman?"

"Adele Pike-Forsyth."

"Oh, wow! The glamour girl of Grade 11! You hit the jackpot!"

"I don't know why she asked me." Mort had found that, with his sister, honesty was the best defence against being filleted by her tongue. "She has her choice of guys in the whole school."

His father tried to head off the harpoon. "I read someplace that beautiful women are often hard up for dates. All the guys assume she's so popular, they don't have a prayer of being her date."

"Oh, Mort isn't her date." (Here it comes: the sibling's verbal knee in the groin.)

"No?" chorused the purblind males.

"Uh-uh. When someone invites you to take her to a movie, you're her date. When she asks you to take her to a dance you're her *escort.*"

" . . . What's the difference?" Mort wanted to know.

Melody raised an eyebrow and exited with: "You'll find out."

The learning experience at which she hinted failed to daunt her gritty brother. Nobody was going to rain on his parade, so long as he was riding Cloud Nine.

It was the longest twenty-four hours of his life, during which he ignored school work, lost interest in eating, and concentrated on the mental video of his putting his arm around the waist of Adele Pike-Forsyth.

That image only enlarged when he went to bed. He had never before had trouble sleeping under a tent. He was able to snatch a few hours by lying on his stomach and thinking hard about taking a bodycheck from Mark Messier.

The next evening, he suffered a more tangible reality check. After showering every part of his eager anatomy, and laying out his Special Occasion shirt and slacks, he found disaster in the bathroom mirror.

A zit. Huge enough, atop his nose, to send shock waves through the rest of his face.

It was as if all his raunchy thoughts about Adele had erupted in one volcanic dome. He half-expected it to start spewing molten lava. By the time he picked up Adele, this Godzilla of pimples would be visible for miles, advertising his pubescent lust.

Frantic, Mort tried to subdue the beast with blasts of baby talc. He merely heightened his resemblance to some Amazon witch doctor.

His last resort was to obscure the obscene object with the nose-clip prescribed by his hockey coach to help him breathe. He just had to hope that Adele would see it as a jock thing.

Mort pillaged his cashbox for cab fare. It represented a lot of hours shovelling the snow off neighbours' walks. After dinner, his father had slipped him a ten-spot, as an investment in his son's sexual orientation. But Mort's evening was still on a tight budget, once he had discarded the pennies to avoid jingling when he danced.

Should I kiss her goodnight? Mort, who liked to think ahead to anticipate problems, was still wrestling with that one when the cab stopped in the driveway of Adele's large house.

"We'll be right back," he told the cabbie, in the innocence of youth.

"She says she'll be out in a minute." The middle-aged man holding a drink did not invite him inside to wait.

"Thank you, sir."

The man — presumably Adele's father — nodded impassively and closed the door.

Mort walked back to the cab. In which he sat, sweating the meter, for eleven minutes before he could jump out and open the door for Adele.

"Sorry," she said. "I didn't expect you to be so on time."

It was his fault. Being fashionably late was one of those social skills not taught at school. Formal education has a lot to learn.

Adele was concentrating on her pocket mirror. "Excuse me," she murmured, "I didn't have time to put on my ring."

Her ring? Mort felt the hair rise on the back of his neck, then subside as he watched Adele slip the small, gold ring into her lower lip.

Sheesh. There goes our kiss goodnight, Mort thought. A surge of passion could cost him a front tooth. But, okay, whatever it takes . . .

At the school, the gym was jumping. Couples crowded the floor, each absorbed in locating rhythm in the school rock band.

When Adele, in a major production, removed her topcoat, Mort was alarmed to see that between her taut black top and her snug leather pants lay an expanse of bare midriff. Her belly button seemed to be winking at him.

And he was supposed to put his arm around that waist, in public? Would this not cause a physical response from him that could get him suspended from the school? And spend the rest of his life hating his father, the instigator of this physical assault?

"Let's go." Adele led him, a lamb to the slaughter, into the tumult of teen saltation. Before he could suggest a low-contact dance, like the Highland fling, she put his arm around her, pressed her body against his, and gazed over his shoulder.

Mort blushed. From head to points farther south. The more he fought it, the more he strained the integrity of his zipper. Quivering, he backed away.

"Sorry," he choked. "Awfully sorry . . . "

"What for?" Adele's radar had zeroed in on her target for the evening, which was twenty feet away and boogeying with her red-head competition. Mort sputtered:

"I thought I . . . stepped on your foot . . . "

"I didn't feel anything." Mort was relieved, yet vaguely disappointed, as she added: "How would you like to get us a drink?"

"Oh, great idea!" Mort gratefully wove to the refreshment bar and lined up for glasses of tranquilized punch.

When he returned to the floor, he saw Adele boogeying, full bore, with Herc Brandon, star quarterback.

Mort found a folding chair that was untaken in the phalanx of wallflowers, and sat there drinking both glasses, while he watched Adele dance dance after dance with the tall heartthrob to whom all things are given.

So Melody was right. He *was* just an escort. Human tofu. The lowest form of social life. Why had he been nerd enough to buy into a dream doomed to turn to nightmare . . . ?

"Mort?"

He looked up to see Jas Mattu, the ample goalie for his hockey team, staring at him with intensity.

"Would you like to dance . . . " Mort cringed at some new horror . . . "with my cousin?"

Mort saw that Jas was shepherding a slight, dusky maiden, who looked as uncomfortable as he felt. "Hey, sure, Jas. But I, uh, basically don't know how to dance."

"That's okay. Rani's parents don't want her to get to like it too much, anyhow. She's just visiting from Bombay — okay?"

As a defenceman, Mort depended on his goalie. "Okay."

Thus did Mort find himelf out on the dance floor again, shuffling his feet to the music, and holding this slim, black-haired person who smelled of jasmine and had enormous brown eyes.

Not having much English, Rani said nearly everything with those eyes. And Mort had no difficulty translating. They said:

"Thank you for being my date."

After their second dance, Mort couldn't even remember what colour Adele's eyes were, or whether they ever said anything except "Me".

Another delight: the gold stud in Rani's nostril provided a mate for the breathing-clip on Mort's nose. Maybe he would have his zit gilded, and one day visit Bombay.

Too soon, Jas reclaimed Rani. Their departure cued Mort to leave the dance too. As he moved out, he saw that Adele and Herc were still slow dancing together, though their faces were starting to show the strain of being the most glamorous couple on the floor.

Mort walked home, still glowing from his contribution to multiculturalism. Under a clear, new, February moon, as bright as Rani's smile, he had to feel good about his first date. Even though, technically, it didn't qualify. He no longer saw his dating a charming girl — especially one wearing a bewitching sari and able to avoid his feet with graceful ease on the dance floor — as the impossible dream.

He had cut it with a girl from India. At fifteen, he had lots of time to win the West.

The Suitor
or Three Stages in a Romance

Barry Mathias

It was spring, and the narrow drive was heady with the smell of hundreds of daffodils. Huge arbutus lined the path, their long, twisting branches defying gravity or entwining the Douglas firs in strong, intimate embraces that had made him blush when "she" had first pointed them out. Ahead was the big house where the object of his passion resided, and where he knew he would be subjected to unending ridicule from the rest of her tiresome family. It did not matter; nothing mattered as long as she was there.

He stopped to polish his black shoes on the back of his trousers. He was wearing his best grey suit, and had pressed the razor-sharp creases himself, using his mother's old steam iron and splashing water onto the material as the hot iron hissed its warning. Perhaps she would not notice the scorch mark on the knee. He straightened his school tie and patted his hair, heavy with Brylcream. There was not a hair out of place, but as he wiped his hand on his clean white handkerchief, he wondered if he had been too generous with the application.

He looked down at the flowers in his hand. Daffodils. Perhaps it had not been a wise choice, but his mother had said it was the thought that counted. His feet crunched loudly on the gravel path as he approached the wide stone steps that led up to the imposing entrance, and he stepped onto the mossy lawn to avoid alerting the dog. However, from inside the hallway the cream Labrador began to bark and hurl itself against the carved door. Now there would be no chance to prepare his introduction.

"Oh, Cripes! It's soppy Steven!" The strident voice of nine-year-old Cleo, the youngest sister.

"Cleopatra! I will not have you saying 'Cripes'! Do grab hold of Wally!" The harassed voice of Mrs. Mintpepper.

"Gwynevere! It's your boyfriend!" The frantic voice of Felicity, the eleven-year-old middle sister.

Steven reached the top step as the door opened a crack, just wide enough to reveal Cleo's pink tongue. He glanced down at his right shoe; there was a thick encrusting of mud on his heel — at least, he hoped it was mud.

"Oh, hello Steven." Mrs. Mintpepper smiled with her mouth, but her eyes reminded him of the nurse who gave injections in the clinic. "How nice to see you again. We didn't expect to see you quite so soon." She stepped back onto a Persian rug to let him enter, as Gwynevere thundered down the stairs. Her long blonde hair was in disarray, and she was desperately trying to adjust her pink flowered dress.

"Gwynevere's changed her dress! Why have you changed your dress?"

"Shut up, Cleo! You're a horrible little brat!"

"Gwynevere! I will not have you saying 'brat'!" cried Mrs. Mintpepper. "Cleo, hold on to Wally!"

"I bought you these," Steven said, holding out the daffodils that had crumpled in his grasp.

"Oh, daffodils! How lovely," said Gwynevere, taking the mangled plants and trying to push Felicity's grinning face out of the way.

At that moment, Wally broke free and threw himself on the ardent suitor. Steven's right foot slipped on the Persian rug; his left foot flew into the air as if he was scoring a goal, and he fell backwards in a tangle of limbs and dog.

As he lay there, gazing up at Gwynevere's startled expression and hearing the unrestrained mirth of "the Brat", the horrified voice of Mrs. Mintpepper roared out: "What is that awful smell?"

♣♣♣

It was summer, and the paved drive was bordered on both sides by fragrant roses, whose heavy perfume emphasized the fecundity of the season. Behind them, the branches of arbutus coiled seductively round the gnarled Douglas firs in a silent passion that echoed his own. The wheels of the red sports car crunched loudly as he braked in front of the stone steps of the house. He gave the engine a final roar, turned off the ignition key with a flourish, and vaulted out of the car. It was an action he had practised during his last month at university.

From an upstairs window, Gwynevere gasped as she saw Steven drive up in his new sports car. He had written his first, tentative letter to her some months before, and she had responded in kind, although somewhat reluctantly: she remembered him as gauche, self-centered, and a ready target for her sisters' ridicule. How the years had changed him! No longer the spotty youth with the Brylcreamed hair who had brought her broken daffodils and trodden dog shit into the Persian rug; he had become an Adonis! His long black hair and lean good looks were intensified by the precision and self-assurance of his every movement.

She was in the act of opening the window, when she saw him vault from the car. His lithe body twisted in the seat, his legs bent up, and he released them together like a single taught spring, high into the air. Gwynevere watched as Steven's muscular arms raised his body over the driver's door, while he twisted round like a gymnast on the parallel beams. Framed in tight blue jeans and a university sweater, he hung suspended in the air for a magical moment, while her heart beat fast and her mouth gaped in wonder.

As he lay prostrate on the ground he was first aware of Cleopatra, the youngest sister; she was sixteen years old and proud of her burgeoning figure. She knelt beside him, and when she leaned over, her ample breasts threatened to burst out of her low-cut blouse.

"Are you okay?" she murmured. Her voice was husky and sensuous. She slipped a warm, naked arm under his head; he could smell lavender.

"I'm . . . I'm not sure," Steven stuttered, unable to avert his gaze from her generous proportions. "My leg hurts. I . . . I think I've twisted something." He tried to sit up. Holding on to Cleopatra for support, he jerked himself into a sitting position and ended up with his face in her bosom, and his arms round her bare shoulders.

"What are you two doing?" The outraged voice of Gwynevere.

"That was quick work, Cleo." The ironic voice of Felicity, the eighteen year old.

"I think you should cover yourself up, Cleopatra." Mrs. Mintpepper's contribution.

Steven released his hold on Cleopatra and sat back on the ground. "I think I've sprained my right ankle," he said sadly. Adopting a brave smile, he tilted his head back in the way he had practised in front of the mirror; it helped to accentuate his jaw line. "Could you help me up, please?"

Cleopatra breathed in deeply, and in the fullness of her newly-acquired womanhood, reached out to help him.

"Leave him to me!" Gwynevere shouted, putting great emphasis on the "me". She lunged forward and pulled Cleopatra's hands away from Steven as he was halfway to standing on his left foot. Caught off balance, he fell backwards and his head hit the side of the car with a crunch like a dropped egg.

There was an ominous hush as the four women surveyed the fallen idol who lay unconscious at their feet.

Mrs. Mintpepper was the first to break the funereal silence. "Girls," she said, "I will not have you fight over Steven. After all, he is only a man." Her lip curled slightly as she added, "And not a very fine example either."

♣♣♣

It was late fall, and the potholed drive was littered with the debris of broken branches from a recent storm. Up above, the huge limbs of the ancient arbutus rested wearily on the rotund trunks of the Douglas firs and, as Steven hastened along the avenue, he felt an increasing sense of the passing of the years. The grand house that he remembered from his youth was a pale shadow of its former self. The paint on the windows was peeling, the carved door was discoloured and sun bleached, and brown weeds sprawled out of the cracks in the once imposing stone steps.

He stopped to calm his breathing and patted his thin, grey hair. The house was as quiet as a mausoleum and he began to doubt if anyone was at home. Taking a deep breath, he yanked his flannel trousers over his belly, adjusted his blazer with the gardening club insignia, and climbed up to the door. There was an old-fashioned bell pull which he tugged cautiously. Nothing happened. He gave it a more robust yank and suddenly the house was filled with a discordant jangling, reminiscent of an air raid warning.

His confidence, which had not been great, evaporated. None of his visits to the Mintpepper house had ever been successful. It was futile to try to reconcile the embarrassments of the past, and he had been unwise to risk his reputation yet again. As he turned to retreat down the steps, the door opened and a slim, silver-haired woman gazed at him inquisitively.

"Ah! Hello, yes . . . I didn't think anyone was at home," he said, conscious of his own awkwardness.

She smiled encouragingly. "Don't I know you?"

"You may remember me. Yes. It was a long time ago. Steven Duckford." He felt his cheeks flush as he glimpsed the worn Persian rug in the hall behind her.

"How nice to see you again, Steven." Her smile emphasized the whiteness of her perfect teeth. "You probably don't remember me. I'm Felicity."

"Oh, yes I do, Felicity," he blurted out, "I remember you very well." She raised her eyebrows in a coquettish way. "What I mean is . . . umm . . . " He did not know how to express himself without, once again, appearing stupid.

Her deep brown eyes smiled at him, and seeing no trace of mockery he gathered his courage. "You see, I've been away for many years."

"I know."

"Oh, do you?" he looked gratified. "I heard you live here by yourself, and I just wanted to reintroduce myself. I wondered if you might still remember me."

"I've never forgotten you, Steven." She spoke with such quiet intensity that his mouth gaped in astonishment.

"You see, I've never forgotten you either," he stammered, "and I wondered if we could . . . "

"I think it would be a lovely idea," she said as she took his hand. "Why don't you come in for some tea?"

The Gene Thief

R.P. MacIntyre

Jode wonders behind his lenses — thick as ice cubes, clamped to his nose — how an insect sees, how they find each other with such ease. They step and place themselves in their horizontal dance as precisely as the edge of a razor blade.

However, his own life has not been sharp.

It has been blunt — a good life, but dull. Jode lives in a flat land where the far sky and fields meet eye to eye. They stare at each other in a kind of hopeless, unblinking stalemate. Everything yawns. Pain isn't much different than pleasure.

The Mullens, my father's family, have survived a long line of rum runners, rear gunners, and high-finance buccaneers. I have an uncle who was busted for growing *cannabis sativa* and an aunt who mounted Everest to its peak. Excitement should form the fabric of at least half of my genetic life.

But all those genes seem to have gone to Clarke Mullen, my cousin. He is a total utter jerk. I admire him.

He walks around with his thumbs hooked into his front pockets and the space between his hips seems suspended by elastic. His face is locked in a perpetual sneer. He drives a black van with darkened windows. He eats hamburgers. He is Not a Nice Person; yet girls find him irresistible. Even Cora used to go with him. I suppose that over the ebb and flow of time, the genetic pool can spill over and get rechanneled.

Or diluted. By people like my mom.

She is the manager of Bulk Fuels at the Co-op. Need I say more?

Dad is an agronomist for the federal government. Semi-arid prairie agriculture. Specialty — brome grass. Plant life. It's the best he can do.

In a way, it's the best I can do too. I don't eat meat. It's not a principled thing with me, I just can't stand the thought of it. There's enough death around. I'm a veggie/pasta/high-carbo kind of guy. Sorry.

Jode is not complaining, really. He accepts things as they are. Reality. Fate. Life is what you get and he has a lot, really — just not a lot of excitement. Bruises occasionally, but no blood. For example, he has an infant brother, Daniel, for whom he would happily lie down and die — not that he plans on doing so soon, because there is also Cora, to whom he would gladly give his heart. Except she's stolen it already.

Cora and I began with long discussions about the meaning of life that somehow concluded in even more lengthy clinches of sprawling limbs, mostly mine, tangled beneath the steering wheel of one of her father's cars. Why talk when you don't have to? Who listens anyway?

My baby brother sits this evening in the middle of the backyard, a gleeful, pudgy Buddha devouring the cosmos. He likes putting stuff into his mouth — anything that fits. Right now it's a fistful of what I hope is only dirt.

"Daniel, don't eat that!"

I pounce on him, then stick my finger in his mouth to seek out the foreign bits. He bites me.

"Daniel! Ouch! Don't bite!"

He looks at me, surprised, like, "Did I do that?" Then flops onto his grubby little paws and paddles away, his white-diapered bum like the south end of a duck. We're waiting for him to walk. But he's not interested. He gets along just fine on all fours. I follow, vertically, from my lofty two-legged height.

I'm on baby patrol tonight. Mom and Dad have gone to some event involving a politician and a dead cow or deer or moose or some other quadrapedal vertebrate. One of them is being barbecued — or roasted, or some combination of the two. However, I'm home, trying to exhaust Daniel so he'll go to sleep when I put him to bed. It's not that I mind but I would rather be doing something else as equally exhausting for me but a lot more fun — with Cora.

Cora has thick, long, red hair, mounds of it that swirl and flare about her head like molten lava. You want to dive into it and drown. I've imagined floundering in it once and came up — tossed spread-eagled onto a sun-bleached beach — gasping, wondering where the hell I was. I respect that hair — it frightens me. She's coming over, soon. Hair and all.

Whenever she's here Cora blinks slower when she looks at Daniel and I wonder if I'm supposed to be jealous. "He's so sweet," she says, which of course is true, but he's also quick. He streaks now for the back door then yanks sharply into Dad's flowerbed — in behind some dahlias. He sits flower head high.

"No, Daniel, don't eat the flowers. Don't eat the . . . "

He holds something shiny and black. It disappears behind his tiny red lips. I step into the flower bed, sink ankle deep in loam, pick him up and probe his mouth, again. This time I feel something. I pull it out. It's a beetle — of the genus, *phyllophaga fusca*, commonly known as a June bug. It has survived Daniel's molarless mouth. I fling it aside.

"Daniel, don't eat bugs, okay?"

He grabs my nose. I honk. He giggles. It's a game we play. He grabs. I honk. He giggles. The only trouble is he can do this forever. Grab. Honk. Giggle. I get impatient after three or four cycles. Time to put the Buddha to bed.

"Okay, Daniel. It's nighty-night time." He should be passed out by the time Cora arrives.

I warm his bottle, change his diaper and snuggle him into his crib. He really is sweet, an angel. He is also what Mom and Dad refer to as their "late" child. A surprise. An accident. I was "the baby" for fifteen years — and we both have a sister who is twenty-five. She has a son who is four which makes Daniel an uncle of someone older than himself. I suspect that at least three of us are miracles of modern contraception.

Cora and I don't use birth control, for the very simple reason we haven't "done it" — technically. It's not that we don't want to, it's just that she's Catholic. She doesn't want to go to hell. Who can blame her? Neither do I. But we have a great time coming close.

It's like a game of chicken, but we play it inside her father's cars.

He owns a dealership, MacLeish Motors, that sells foreign, exotic, *little* cars. It's been in a succession of these that we have tangled. I said one night that I wished he sold vans and she bit me on the ear, hard.

"Ow!" I said.

"I'm sorry," she said, "I didn't mean to."

But she had.

Daniel the cherub is sleeping. I have taken a high dive and plunged into Cora's hair. We are downstairs on the rec room couch, supposedly watching a movie. The blue flicker of the TV mumbles behind us. Neither of us knows what precisely is on, something with much water or sky, and guys with guns, in boats or helicopters. We are quite busy groping for body parts. Some of which seem to have grown achily large.

Cora suddenly breaks apart. Becomes rigid. "What's that?" she says. Her hair is askew, her lips are blurred. She looks ravishing. She is ravishing. Mind you, I've removed my glasses.

My mouth tries to make a word. "Wha . . . " I croak.

"A sound," she says.

We both listen.

Nothing.

I run my fingers through her hair. At this precise second I am thinking: what goes on in their minds? I know what goes on in my mind — nothing. All thought has been pushed aside by exquisite, utter, and sheer physical delight. Our lips begin to meet — when there *is* a sound. An unmistakable creak — series of creaks — upstairs.

"Does Daniel walk?" Cora whispers.

"He didn't at bedtime." I grasp for my glasses.

We rise from the couch, tucking in and buttoning our clothes. We tiptoe up the stairs.

We peer into the kitchen. Nothing.

We peer into the living room. Nothing.

Daniel's room! I dash. He lies, angelic, bum high.

"I guess it was nothing," I say, coming out of Daniel's room, "unless we suddenly have ghosts in here."

"Ghosts with muscles," she says.

"What do you mean?"

"Your sound system is gone."

And there in the cabinet, where the sound system lived, is a hole — big, blank, and empty.

The next morning while the police are here, I am eagerly, diligently reconstructing the previous evening. I am a sleuth. I find a footprint near the back door. The thieves — there had to be more than one — entered there. One of the detectives, Detective Swan, makes a plaster cast of the print. "It might help," he says. But I am a lying sleuth. In my reconstructed evening, Cora and I are the rapt audience of a TV movie whose volume is cranked to the ceiling.

"What was it called?" asks Detective Swan.

"What?"

"The movie you were watching?"

"Jeez, I can't remember, Officer. Or sir. Or . . . " I don't know what to call him.

"You can't remember?"

"It escapes me at the moment."

He probes me with his eyes. A slow, calculating probe — for the ancestors in my genes.

"What was your girlfriend's name?"

"Cora, Officer. Cora MacLeish. She was with me all evening," I say in her defense.

"I know. That's why I want to talk to her. Maybe *she* can remember the name of the movie."

Oh God! He thinks we did it.

"Yes, right. Of course. Maybe *she* can remember." I utter a weak, false laugh that sounds like I am clearing my throat. I realize at this moment it's quite possible that I am going to jail — innocent.

Innocence, of course, is relative. And Daniel is truly beyond reproach. My parents go beyond the obvious to remind me.

"What if he'd been taken, Jode? Then what? How would you feel then?" says Mom.

"I'd feel bad."

"You'd feel *bad*?"

"I'd feel worse than bad, I mean, I feel bad now."

"I hope so," says Dad.

I'll feel worse in jail though. Not only are the CD player, turntable, amplifier, and speakers gone, but so are a host of other things: a camera, a pair of binoculars, some of Mom's jewelry, the microwave oven, and of all the stupid things, the coffee grinder.

Things may have gone more smoothly if the coffee grinder was still around.

Both my parents are hopeless coffee addicts. They need it in the morning like Daniel needs milk. It's their lifeblood. A day without coffee is like the sun without light, like water without wet.

Like Cora without hair.

She calls, wanting to meet at her church.

"Why at your church?"

"So God is our witness."

"Why do we need a witness?"

"Because, idiot." She hangs up.

I trudge seven blocks to a red brick building with a steeple on top. Her church. St. Jerome's. I knew a Jerome in band. He played clarinet till his girlfriend hit him in the mouth with a bowling ball the night that they broke up. He said it was an accident. How do you accidentally hit someone in the mouth with a bowling ball?

I am thinking about split lips and blood when I walk into the church.

Cora's got a haircut. She's as bald as a bowling ball. I feel like I've been hit in the mouth.

"What happened?" I ask.

"The police came and talked to me."

"No, to your hair," I say.

"Oh, I cut it off."

"I can see that. Why?"

"For Lent."

"For *Lent?* Who's Lent?"

"It's not a who, it's a what."

And she explains to me how in her church they have this time called Lent where you're supposed to give something up — something you especially like. So she shaved her head.

"God," I say. Her ears look big. And her nose. Her eyes used to look like they fit into her face. Now they look *attached* to it.

"What's the matter?" she asks.

"Nothing," I say.

"You don't like it, do you?"

"Don't like what?"

"It doesn't matter because I'm giving you up too."

"For *Lent*?"

"Lent is over," she says, adding, "It's not you I'm giving up — it's sex."

"Sex?" I say. I'm truly confused.

"My period's late."

"Your period's late?"

"Stop repeating everything I say."

"Why is your period late?"

"Guess," she says.

I am guessing. I mean we haven't done it — technically — unless one of my sperm was an incredibly good swimmer, through at least one set of clothes.

"How could it be late? We haven't done it — technically."

"Well, either I'm the virgin frickin' Mary or we *have* done it — technically."

There was that once where we kind of, sort of started to — but we really didn't get totally naked where you need to get totally naked. I mean, I *know* these things. I study *insects.* They don't have to take their pants off.

"Do you know for sure?"

"Of course I know for sure. Women know these things." She turns away from me, her head down. She might break into tears.

I am suddenly terrified. That all this fun could lead to this terror doesn't seem fair. I don't know what to do. I reach for her hand. Perhaps some tenderness.

"Don't touch me," she says.

I withdraw. "Whatever happens, I'll stick with you," I say.

"Maybe I don't want you to stick with me."

"What?" Again, I reach for her. She looks beautiful once more.

"Don't touch me!"

"What's with you, am I a leper or something?"

"You might be. You're skin is falling off."

I look at my hands. She's right. My skin *is* falling off. In flakes.

I've gone to the doctor. The disease I have is some kind of *candidiasis*, a fungal infection. Skin is not only flaking off my hands, it's falling off my feet too. I'm apparently allergic to yeast. Yeast is in *everything*. There's nothing to eat, except meat. I don't eat meat. My parents eat meat. Let them.

I grow weak, gaunt, spectral.

My mom makes me wear bandages on my hands. She won't let me hold Daniel. We can't play our little game of grab, honk, giggle. "Don't touch him!" she says. Daniel doesn't get it. He sits on the floor, his arms outstretched. Pick me up, he's saying.

"I can't, Daniel. Mom thinks you'll get leprosy."

Daniel starts crying and he seldom cries.

"There, there," says Mom, lifting him to her hip.

He sobs big noisy tears that splash on the floor. I have never noticed that a baby's tears are as large as a grown-up's. He is so small and helpless, and I am such a big goof.

"What are *you* bawling about?" Mom asks me.

"Am I crying?" I sob.

"Buckets," she says.

"I don't know," I say. And I don't.

The parts of me that are not flaking away are covered in strange white welts.

A break in the theft case — the police have identified the plaster-cast footprint.

It's mine.

I go to bed.

Let them come and pry me loose. I'm not moving from here. Here I can do no damage. Here none can be done to me. Why is this happening? Just who is responsible? God? The *Fates*?

"Go pick on somebody who deserves it!" I scream. "Somebody who starts wars, somebody who kills and maims, somebody who drives around in a black van seducing people, somebody who advises the use of pesticides to wreck the earth, somebody who pollutes the atmosphere with the stink of burnt fossil fuels that punch holes in the ozone layer at both the north and the south pole, somebody who . . . "

Then it occurs to me.

Maybe this is a test. Maybe God or The Fates or whoever it is, is testing the mettle of the human species. Maybe he, she, or it is trying to see just how tough we are, how malleable we are in the face of great, insurmountable odds. And I am the testee. Does the testee have any testicles?

"Ha!" I laugh recklessly. "Hurl at me, you Fates, everything you've got." I shake my fist at the ceiling of my room. Something falls off my arm. More skin? No, it's small and black. It's moving. *They* are moving.

Shit. There are bugs in my bed.

Cimex lectularius — bed bugs. They are a flat, wingless, bloodsucking, hemipterous insect. That would explain the welts.

Something in me snaps, released — an anger, a rage. It's time to plot revenge, death — *insecticide.* I start slow with those I can see, one at a time. I pinch them between my fingers, snapping off their crusty pincered heads. Those I find pop red with blood — my blood. The rest have scuttled into the folds of the bedsheets, blankets, and pillows, and are tucked away tight.

Dad has a small workshop in the basement — next to my room. It's where he keeps his poisons. No invertebrate has ever survived our lawn. I make a little cocktail: lindane, trichlorofon, ronnel, and some pyrethrins to do the trick. I just about forget the diazinon.

I tear off the sheets, the cases, the blankets. I stuff them into the washing machine. I pour bleach over them. I pour soap. I pour a half-litre of malathion. There is no *disinfectant* cycle. Just *heavy-duty, hot.* I turn it on.

I yank my mattress from its frame. I spray it with my cocktail. I spray both sides. I put a damp towel over my mouth. I remove my PJs. I spray them and the whole damned room. The delightful smell of death. I seal the bedroom door with packing tape.

Through all this is a brilliant clarity, a realization: there is one life I can control — *mine.*

I shower, then go upstairs in my housecoat. I grab a bagel from the bread box.

"What are you doing?" asks Mom.

"I'm eating," I say.

"You can't eat that," she says.

"I can eat whatever I want. I am *carpying the diem,*" I say. "Where's Daniel?"

"You're what?"

Daniel has heard me. He crawls into the kitchen and breaks into a huge, shiny-cheeked grin. I pick him up.

"Put him down," says Mom.

Daniel grabs my nose.

"'Honk.' Daniel and I are going for a truck ride, aren't we, Daniel?"

He giggles.

"Put him down," Mom says again. "You're not dressed."

"And you have a lousy job that puts holes in the ozone."

"What? What . . . " she sniffs. "What's that smell?"

"Diazinon."

"Diazinon?"

"I used all the malathion."

"What do you want with malathion?"

"There are bed bugs in the basement, that's why I'm taking Daniel out."

I head for the door.

"What? Where? Wha . . . " she splutters. "You can't go out like that."

"I have to. My clothes are in my room."

I'm on my way to Cora's in Dad's dirty red pickup. He's at a soil salinity conference. The grass man has to know the salt of his earth. I need to know mine. Daniel is strapped in his baby seat looking pensive.

"What's the matter?" I ask.

He reaches a little hand in my direction. He wants to grab my schnozz. I lean my head closer to him so he can reach. Unfortunately, I am also turning the steering wheel. Daniel doesn't get to grab because there is suddenly a loud "thump".

I have collided with the car alongside of me, and although collide may be too strong a word, it is definitely not a caress. I crank the wheel back. My heart is somewhere between my ear lobes. I glance beyond Daniel into the next lane where red and blue lights are already ablaze.

I've hit a cop car.

After we've pulled over and have assessed the damage — none to me, but I've left a red crease in the cop's rear fender and have sprung the cruiser's trunk lid — the officer is taking down my license information.

I am trying to appear nonchalant in my housecoat, like this is normal dress for me, and the cop is giving me a very peculiar look. It's one of those don't-I-know-you-from-somewhere looks. And he does, because I suddenly recognize him too. It's Detective Swan, or should I say, former Detective Swan, because he is out of uniform now and has either suffered some sort of demotion or is moonlighting. We are standing at the rear of his car.

"It was all my fault, Officer," I say. "My little brother wanted to grab my nose and . . . "

I pause, gazing into Officer Swan's trunk. In it is a stereo system, plus an assortment of other household goods. They look extremely familiar.

Officer Swan notes my observation. "I was on my way to your place to return this stuff," he says. "Quite a coincidence, isn't it?"

"Yes," I say, "except I live the other way." I point.

"Right, I know that," he says with excessive cheerfulness. "I was just going, you know, around the other way, the long way. And you're obviously going somewhere really important. Why don't I escort you?" He is trying to close the trunk lid.

"What about the dent in your fender?" I ask.

"Dent? I backed into a fire hydrant," he says with a big, fake smile. "All in the line of duty."

Officer Swan's cruiser departs from Cora's house with an annoyed little chirp. Fresh-ground coffee will again appear at home.

I heave Daniel onto my hip and we grab, honk, and giggle our way to Cora's front door. I place Daniel's pudgy finger onto the doorbell.

We hear a chime, then a stirring within the house.

Daniel becomes still. He rests, contemplative in his sweet way, waiting

Cora opens the door. She wears a dark, stubbled fuzz where her hair used to be.

"God," she says. "What happened to you?"

I've forgotten what *I* look like — the wrath of God, welted and flaking, my housecoat flapping in the breeze. I tell her about the bed bugs and how they lay dead or dying in my basement room. "But who cares about that?" I segue. "Say hi to Daniel."

"Hi, Sweetie," she says, then takes his hand and leads us — with me still holding him — into the garage. We weave between her father's cars, the insides of which

I am intimately familiar with, to emerge onto the patio. I set Daniel down to range. A whole new yard to explore.

"Jodie, I have to tell you something," she says.

"Good. So do I." And here I know I should pause with great deliberation, but I don't. I just blurt it out. "I want to marry you, or you to marry me. Whichever you prefer."

Her mouth hangs open. She closes it, then swallows. "I really like you, Jode, but . . . " She stalls again.

"Yes, you like me, but . . . "

"I *am* pregnant, you know."

"I know that," I say.

"But you're not the father."

I stare at the stubble on her head. It's a beautiful head. I can still remember the lava. My heart, at this moment — even though it's not mine — is bursting.

"It's your cousin," she says. "Clarke."

"Clarke?" My heart. Explodes.

But not Clarke's black van.

It rocks and rocks, then teeters and tips, acquiver. Spent. A big black June bug, its feet in the air. *Phyllophaga fusca.* The vision passes.

"When?" I say.

"When*ever*," she says.

"Even after we started going out?"

"Especially after."

"Oh . . . that's why you cut your hair."

She turns her head away.

"You can't be ugly to me."

"Yeah, but *you* think *bugs* are beautiful."

"They are." I push my glasses back up my nose. "In their way."

Daniel suddenly squeals, filling the air with delight, not able to contain some great, secret joy. Cora and I both turn to watch him slapping the grass with his palms. We're thankful for the diversion as he returns from the lawn to join us on the patio.

Cora meanders closer, wanting to help him climb. However, Daniel is intent on doing this alone. It's a brief step. He plants his hands then raises a chubby leg that overbalances the upper half of his short body and he suddenly tips, banging his head on the concrete.

He howls, and as joyous as his sound was moments ago, it is now wretched with pain.

Cora reaches and pulls him up "There, there," she says, lifting him to her lips. She kisses Daniel's head as he wails. "Aunty Cora will make it better," she says and kisses him again, his tears splashing like rain. *Aunty Cora will make it better.*

I join this inexplicable huddle, two of us kissing the sobbing third.

Then two of us, *balancing on a razor's edge,* kiss each other. Listening.

Stealing the sharp, keen pain of being alive.

I Need My Privacy

Janice Scott

They took the cubicle doors off in the girls' washroom at our high school again. Well, all but one, that is. The winning candidate's platform in the last election for student council president was *Bare Bums No More, We Need A Door,* but I guess it didn't do any good. The problem is that the washroom cubicles had become a prime location for cigarette smoking (and on occasion other types of smoking as well). I have to admit that it was getting difficult actually to use the washroom the way it was intended. The school administration felt the doorless solution would remedy the problem, when in fact it has just meant there were always about eight girls in that one cubicle with a door, smoke puffing upwards amidst giggling and a liberal use of four-letter words. It was like those pictures you see in books of world records of students squished into a Volkswagen.

On the bright side, it cut down on profane graffiti, because I suppose it is difficult to write when your body is jammed behind a toilet. But I don't know for sure. I have only been a casual observer and not a bona fide member of this elite group of "toilet tokers", as I call them. I haven't really tried to join either. I am what is called a "nerd", a "browner", or the latest unfortunate label, a "loser", because among other things, I like to brush my teeth in the washroom. Very uncool. There is a large number of us in this category. Well, not girls who brush their teeth in the school washroom, but those of us who just want to use the washroom in the traditional way. Safety in numbers. Secretly, I have to say I don't mind that I have never really been swayed by peer pressure. But this attitude does not gain one many friends, at least not until the latter years of high school.

In the meantime, a solution to my personal hygiene dilemma had to be found. I was not about to start using a cubicle that has no door. I did once in a bus station in Alberta, but I was thousands of kilometres away from my home in Ontario and there was very little chance of seeing anyone I knew. Besides, it was urgent. I suppose I could have waited until the smoke cleared and used the cubicle that did offer privacy, but that hardly seemed like a practical solution. The bulk of my lunch period would have been spent waiting in line for a toilet that had footprints all over it. It had become apparent that I would just have to go elsewhere.

I attend a downtown high school now, having switched last year from a scholarly suburban school when I decided I wanted to take plumbing. (At this point, it seems appropriate to point out the irony of my present dilemma.) So I left the academia scene for what they call "tech", and with the exception of the fact that there are gaps in the facilities, it has proven to be a happy decision for me. I have made many friends of different economic and racial backgrounds, my closest friend being Teresa. The school is located only a few short blocks from the business and shopping core of the city. So the other day, after I had eaten my lunch in the cafeteria, I decided to walk downtown and look for a washroom with cubicle doors.

The weather was lovely and clear, which was more than you could say for the air in the girls' washroom. Teresa saw me going out the front door of the school and caught me before I could make my exit.

"Hey, Heather! Where are you going?" she yelled like a hog caller.

"Good grief, Teresa, you don't need to yell at me! What do you want?" I immediately felt badly for snapping at her, but she had caught me off guard. Usually, I told Teresa everything, but I really had no good way of explaining what I was going to do. I felt my face flush, even though she didn't know what I was up to. I had to think fast. I decided to fake it. "I'm out of solder. I thought I might go over to the hardware and pick some up," I said.

"What are you talking about?" Teresa asked, scrunching up her face like a wet cloth.

"You know, that stuff I use to stick water pipes together in plumbing? Well, I should get going. I'll see you in history class, okay?" I responded quickly before she had any time to think about how nutty I sounded. I ran out the door and down the sidewalk, wondering if I had enough money to buy some solder so I wouldn't feel so bad about what I told Teresa. I decided I would worry about that later.

I thoroughly enjoyed the fresh air and, at the risk of sounding vain, I also loved the occasional opportunity to glance at myself in the large expanses of glass in storefront windows. With my shoulders back, I could flick my hair and be a really famous fashion model in a shampoo advertisement, if only for one fleeting moment. But back to the task at hand. My goal was to find facilities in a public building; slightly luxurious would be a bonus.

I have to admit I had a bit of an advantage. I have a little sister who, at five years of age, is eleven years younger than I. She is often put in my charge and as a result, I am familiar with every restroom in the province. I knew of one in particular at the Tourist Information Bureau on the main street. It was lovely. I was there one day last summer selecting brochures and other freebies with my sister while my mother shopped at a nearby department store. I guess I looked like a "local" because I was asked many questions and met a very nice couple from Bath, England. Or maybe it was Bath, Ontario. I'm not exactly sure, but they were very clean, anyways. I remembered where the Tourist Information Bureau was, so I turned the corner at Water Street. I was glad that it wasn't too far because I didn't want to be late getting back to school for afternoon classes.

The Tourist Information Bureau is located in an historical building, the old city hall. There is a new city hall now. It's further up the main street, a modern, angular building covered in windows that sparkle like cubic zirconia in the midday sun. Despite that, I like the old city hall building better.

It was still early springtime, so there had not as yet been many tourists in the city. When I opened the door to the Tourist Information Bureau, a bell tinkled to announce the arrival of visitors. The sound of it made me cringe. I soon realized that I was the only one there and I was a bogus tourist at that. Luckily, though, no one was out at the information desk and I slipped by unnoticed into the back hallway where I knew the ladies' room was. I tiptoed carefully on the creaky wood floors, trying hard not to make any noise. It was dark and warm and I inhaled a whiff of lemon oil soap. I became a bit overwhelmed, not by lemon oil soap, but by self doubt. It passed when my sweaty hand grasped the brass handle of the washroom door. Quietly, I disappeared into my own private feminine sanctuary.

It was as I had remembered. Heavenly. The delicate scent of lavender enveloped me like a meadow of wildflowers. Antique brass lamps glowed over the oval mirrors and porcelain sinks. The whole room was done in a satiny rose wallpaper that surrounded me like a soft pillow. I was alone. Alone with my thoughts. I almost left, but then my reflection told me I shouldn't just yet.

I had come prepared. I pulled my butane curling iron out of my knapsack and set it down carefully on the ceramic countertop. Next I retrieved my travel toothbrush and toothpaste so that I could brush my teeth. I had all the travel accessories and for a moment I pretended I was actually on holiday somewhere. Bath, England would do nicely. I felt self-indulgent and pampered, in my own luxurious loo with cubicle doors. When I was finished, I stealthily slipped back out, barely noticed by a woman who was now visible in a back office. She waved and called out, "Can I help you with anything, dear?"

"Oh no, thank you," I replied, and smiled meekly. Back out in the sunlight, reality hit me and I looked at my watch. I had only ten minutes to get back to the school and I started to run — which ruined my freshly curled hair. I remembered that I hadn't bought any solder.

This routine continued to work well for a week. It became a rejuvenating break in the school day, a sort of beauty spa experience, complete with exercise when you include the walk there and back. Soon I found myself not only brushing my teeth and curling my hair, but washing my face and reapplying my makeup as well. My knapsack bulged with beauty aids. I also happily learned that my anonymity was safe for a while when I discovered that volunteers provided the staff for the Tourist Information Bureau. Each day brought a new face, usually an elderly woman, well dressed and eager to answer the questions of real tourists, not bathroom junkies.

"Heather, you look great these days. Share your secret, will you?" Teresa remarked around the third day. I felt guilty that I was leading this secret lunch life and not telling Teresa about it. I felt fortunate that she had forgotten about the solder, but my instincts told me the jig would soon be up. My instincts were right. It happened at the end of the first week which was a relief. The burden of a guilty conscience as a result of deceiving not only Teresa but also the dear ladies at the Tourist Information Bureau was becoming too much.

"Heather, I'm so depressed. You look gorgeous and fresh every day, all day. You make me look like so bad," she whined. I thought for a moment about her comments. Did that mean that I was hideously unattractive prior to my new noon-hour beauty regimen? That she only had become friends with me because of superficial flaws that, by comparison, made her look fantastic? Our friendship could possibly be in jeopardy and I knew it was time to fess up.

"Well, Teresa, you're never going to believe this," I started, "but I have been going to the ladies' washroom at the Tourist Information Bureau downtown for about a week now. At lunchtime." There was a lot of commotion around us because we were standing in the hallway between classes, but Teresa didn't notice any of it. She was staring at me, her eyes wide, her mouth open, her brow furrowed. "Please don't tell a soul. I'd be the butt of jokes around here forever," I blurted out, suddenly aware of the terrible risk I had just taken by sharing this information.

After an uncomfortable long pause, she finally spoke. "Heather, you are one weird chick. Why on earth are you going to the Tourist Information Bureau? Isn't that, like, supposed to be for tourists and stuff?" she asked.

"Well, yes, I guess so. But I just didn't want to wait for the only cubicle in the girls' washroom that has a door," I said.

"Heather, they put them back three days ago. Too many students were sneaking into the staff washroom. Didn't you know?" she asked, and then she pursed her lips to keep from laughing.

I felt like an idiot. I was speechless. Teresa read my embarrassment well. "Listen, I promise I won't tell anybody about this if you'll take me with you today. I want to check this place out, man," she said. "Maybe it'll work for me too!"

"Okay," I agreed. "I always go after I eat lunch in the cafeteria. We'll go then."

"That solves one mystery for me. I wondered what you could be doing with so much solder!" Teresa said and she walked away. She started laughing out loud. I couldn't blame her.

We ate lunch together as we usually do, but for the last little while Teresa had been letting me get away so I could go buy more solder. This time we left together. The weather was lovely, so we wouldn't need coats. Teresa started to head for the door. "Hang on, Teresa; I have to go to my locker and get my knapsack," I said.

"What do you need your knapsack for?" she asked.

"You'll see," I answered. I was starting to feel just a little more confident about this. I pulled my knapsack full of beauty accessories out of my locker and swung it on my back in one smooth move.

"Have you got enough stuff in there, Heather?" Teresa asked, snickering. It was true, I could hardly carry it anymore, but I would just have to be cool. We walked outside and down the sidewalk, basking in the warm spring sun. I didn't bother checking my reflection in the storefront windows, for fear of being caught and being totally rejected. I knew I was on shaky ground here. I'm sure I saw her looking at herself once, though. We turned at Water Street.

"Okay, where is this place?" Teresa asked.

"Right there," I answered, pointing up the street like I really knew what I was doing. I could see that there were quite a few people going in ahead of us, and I breathed a sigh of relief. I knew that we would be lost in the masses, just two more tourists who would remain nameless. The tinkling bell announced our arrival as expected, but no one noticed. We strutted by the displays of glossy brochures, maps, and guidebooks. I recognized the volunteer behind the counter, but she was occupied answering queries of a genuine nature for someone who was having difficulty speaking English. I directed Teresa down the narrow, dark hallway, and then finally into my secret refuge. I don't know what I had expected, but she didn't gasp or slap her chest in euphoric surprise. Instead she was quiet, probably wondering what the heck was wrong with her friend.

"Not bad. It's very private," she said. It was true. Despite all the people who were there, no other women were coming in. But there was a lot of commotion on the other side of the door. Voices floated down the hall, creating a hum that reverberated through the slats in the wood door. We primped and fussed for a while, not speaking, just enjoying the bond of our friendship. Teresa was pleasantly surprised by the results and she glowed like a model on the catwalk. I looked at my watch and saw that it was time to pack up and head back.

"You know, Heather, this was wicked," Teresa said. She smiled, turned, and opened the door. But the hallway wasn't dark anymore. In fact it was lit up like a movie set. We walked out to where the information counter was and, to our horror, were confronted by a television camera. The woman with the luscious blonde hair was not the Tourist Information Bureau volunteer.

"Ho chi mama!!" we said together. It was Linda Darling, the local television news reporter who, at that moment, turned and started speaking to the camera.

"Good afternoon, everyone. This is Linda Darling reporting for the Noon News, live from the Tourist Information Bureau. Today we are talking to tourists who are visiting our fair city to find out firsthand what brings them here and what they have enjoyed the most!" she said. "Oh, look, here come some young tourists now," she gushed. And she turned to face us. "Girls, tell us, where are you from? What made you two young ladies visit the Tourist Information Bureau today? What have you enjoyed the most? By the way, you two look fabulous!" And with that, she pushed the microphone in our faces.

I thought I was going to faint. In fact, I wished I would faint. But I didn't. We both just stood there stunned. There was a long, long, hideous pause.

"Girls?" she repeated. By now all the eyes of the legitimate tourists were on us, their ears waiting eagerly for our response, probably hoping for some tips on what they should see and do. I didn't think before I spoke because I suspect my conscience was now in control. My words just poured out.

"My name is Heather and this is Teresa and we're not tourists, we live right here and go to high school about two blocks away and we are at the Tourist Information Bureau to use the washroom because our school washroom has cubicles with no doors, well they do now, but they didn't used to and we're really sorry and we have enjoyed the washrooms the most."

Ms. Darling looked thoroughly confused and tilted her head like a cocker spaniel. She took a moment before she spoke in a very, very slow manner. "Thank you, girls. What a most interesting and surprising answer," she said. I could see the volunteer behind the counter put her hand to her mouth.

"Well, have a nice day everyone," Teresa said unexpectedly. And then we headed for the hills, as they say in the movies. We bolted out the door, the bell nearly falling from its hook, and down the street, dodging shoppers and office workers. We didn't stop until we got back to the school. Our fresh faces had wilted quickly, our makeup was running like watercolour paints, but I didn't care. It wasn't important.

"Hey, Heather, you forgot to buy your solder," Teresa called as she walked down the hall to her locker.

"I don't need it; things will hold together without it," I answered. Teresa laughed. I turned to go to my locker so I could go unload my heavy knapsack, once and for all.

Obedience

Shelley A. Leedahl

"Tell me about one of the strangest moments in your life." Paula jerks on her Dalmatian's leash and yanks him back in by her side. "Albert! Heel!"

"Let's see," Kailey says, thinking. She cuffs her cocker spaniel lightly beneath the chin to stop him from nipping at her bare ankles. "There was that time I went to midnight mass. I'm not Catholic, but when I was thirteen I went through a phase where I thought it'd be romantic to be a nun."

Paula stops and raises her eyebrows. The dogs tangle. Kailey and Paula let them sniff each other's butts for an embarrassing thirty seconds, then wrench them apart.

Kailey continues. "When everyone else started lining up for Communion, I joined right in. I was fully expecting a tiny square of store-bought bread — United Church, all the way. When the priest stuck this disc thing in my mouth I spit it out into the altar boy's plate. Thought it was cardboard."

"That's good," Paula says. "I had a weird moment at my wedding. My husband dropped the ring."

"Which husband was that?" Kailey asks.

"Number one."

"Prophetic, wouldn't you say?"

Paula turns and smiles. Albert craps on the spot.

It's dusk and the human/canine foursome are strolling along Saskatoon's Spadina Crescent, with the muddy river on one side and some of the city's grandest homes on the other. They met in puppy obedience school. Paula thought Kailey was far older than her "seventeen . . . well, almost eighteen" years, and Kailey would never have guessed that Paula was "a worldly twenty-four," and a remarried divorcee to boot. They had coffee, swapped phone numbers and sarcastic remarks about their instructor, the other dogs, and their owners. They've become unlikely friends.

The obedience classes ended weeks ago. The dogs, both now in their adolescence, have had sufficient time to forget everything they learned. Paula still tries. She carries a little plastic bag of liver cake: foul-smelling treats which she pops into her dog's mouth when he flukes and sits before crossing a street. In her pocket, a larger plastic bag. The liver cakes pass right through him.

The Dalmatian sprints ahead and Kailey drags Winston, her lagging spaniel, to catch up. "So . . . is it any better the second time around?" She has a vested interest in all matters related to love. Her own two-year relationship, like her dog, is lagging. Mike, her boyfriend and intended, still thinks everything's peachy. He doesn't know how many metaphorical miles these walks with Paula have taken Kailey. He thinks he has everything figured out. They graduate from grade twelve this month, get engaged same time next year. Sure, it's a little young, he agrees, but they *know* they're meant to be together. He believes that their lives fit together like pieces of a puzzle, and when the final piece is snapped into place, the picture will include Mike and his law degree; a split-level in the 'burbs; two angelic children; Winston, the well-trained cocker spaniel; and the proverbial white picket fence built high enough so that the dog can't escape. Kailey is in the picture, too, but you really have to look for her. She's peeking out from behind the kitchen curtains, looking a smidgen tired. She's just pulled a loaf of bread from the oven, and now she's about to iron Mike's shirts.

Kailey sighs.

"Not better, just different," Paula says, stealing her young friend from the reverie. They spy an approaching Doberman and his sleek, navy-suited owner. Both are smiling and showing off their sharp, white teeth.

Kailey reins Winston in tight. "How so?"

"Well, when you first get married, on the one hand you're all caught up in love everlasting . . . "

The dogs suddenly detour into knee-high grass, jerking their humans along behind them. Beyond the grass lies a wooded slope where you can make-believe that you've left the city behind. A hiking trail snakes through the brush, then there's another small rise before the metre-width of beach and the South Saskatchewan River. The pair have been warned not to take their dogs to the bank. The beavers are restless; more than one dog's gone down. Kailey's spaniel yaps as something slithers through the grass. She snaps his lead off and Winston leaps forward. Paula follows Kailey to a park bench. Albert complains; Paula relents. The liberated dogs play tag.

Kailey jumps back on the thought train. "You were saying?"

Paula gives her a vacant, hazel-eyed stare.

"About love everlasting . . . "

"Oh, yes." Paula rubs her Achilles tendon. She knows she needs better shoes. "At first you're all wrapped up in love everlasting, but after a year or two, give or take, 'til death do us part' begins to stretch before you like an emotional desert."

An emotional desert. Kailey nods, like she knows the landscape well. She loves these heart-to-hearts with her much more experienced friend. She convinces herself that she won't make the same mistakes that Paula and her own, homemaker mother have made. Domesticity sucks. It's the eve of the millennium, she thinks. Everything's changed since her parents swapped vows. Women keep their own names, choose to be single parents. They have careers and families. She's about to leap into a more enlightened, more equitable, adult world. So she'll likely marry Mike. He's not *that* bad — he can actually be quite charming — and at least he has goals. Besides Mike, she's not sure what else her future holds. She's got time to figure it all out, doesn't she?

"My mom said, 'Don't marry him if you have any doubts.' But who doesn't?" Paula bends to tie her shoelace.

Kailey squirms. Is she that easy to read?

Paula continues. "First it was one little thing that bugged me, like leaving his dirty socks in the living room. Then it was something else.

"He never put the milk away . . . " Kailey thinks aloud, imagining her future as the lawyer's wife.

"Yeah, something like that. All those things kept getting under my skin . . . "

Kailey thinks of ticks, their dogs in the brush.

"I kept saying to myself: this marriage has to work. At least until we've used all the wedding gifts. Like the clock. I swore I'd stay with him until the damn clock broke. And the dishes, and the punch bowl." Paula swats at a mosquito near her ear.

Kailey slouches, rests one brown arm along the back of the bench. "I hear ya'."

"Well, pretty soon I found I was spending most of my time fixing up all the things he'd undone and I realized I wasn't having any fun. So I said, that's it. It's over."

"Just like that?"

"Yep."

"Okay," Kailey asks,"what about round two?"

"Same thing, only I was so desperate, I *am* so desperate to make this one work, that I ignore a lot of the bullshit. I just get miserable. Spend a lot of time away. Go to art openings . . . "

" . . . and dog obedience classes," Kailey finishes.

"Bingo." Paula's voice goes flat.

Kailey wants to say something, anything, encouraging, but this is one of those moments when she's acutely aware that their lives are still years and planets apart. Or are they? What if Mike wants a wife like his mother, the veritable handmaid? The guys in that family — three perfectly capable sons and a husband — don't lift a finger to help the poor woman. She still cleans their rooms, does all their laundry, makes their school lunches and cuts the crusts off their bread. Worse, Kailey thinks, Mike's parents have separate bedrooms. What's up with that?

"The dogs!" Paula blurts, reminding Kailey that they've disappeared. They call. They whistle. They tramp through bushes and trees. There's splashing: wild splashing.

"Albert!"

"Winston!"

They crash toward the terrible sound, stumbling over beaver-chewed logs and ducking beneath lazy branches to get to the river's edge. Kailey blows out a sandal.

The dogs are intact. Wet, but safe. Breathless, Kailey plops onto the sand. She pretends to cry. Winston is bewildered. He skulks over to her side."That's a good boy!" she says, remembering the official phrase from class. The dog shakes, soaking her.

Paula leaves a trail of liver cake along the bank and teases her Dalmatian from the water. "Good dog! Yes!"

When they finally have the sopping hounds snapped again to their leads, all four continue along the hiking trail. The strapless sandal's an annoyance; Kailey slap-drags her left foot. Bushes canopy overtop of them, blocking what light the sun offers. The traffic on Spadina is muffled by the tangle of straight and fallen trees that climb the slope. We're invisible down here, Kailey thinks. An occasional bird sends a greeting and there's the rustling of the dogs, nosing along the path, the crunching of twigs beneath their own feet, but it's the silence that seizes her attention. "It's getting dark," she whispers. Her words are three small stones dropped from a bridge. "Should we be down here?"

"It's not that . . . "

A bell brring-brrings behind them. "On your left!" A tightly-muscled cyclist in black spandex shorts weaves between them, head like a bullet in his grey helmet. Kailey's breath gets stuck in her throat. The dogs beg to run.

"Didn't hear him coming," Paula says. "Heel!"

They abandon the dirt trail for the safety of the sidewalk and continue north toward the weir, where signs warn pedestrians that the steep cement embankment is a restricted area. They stop to watch the pelicans bob in the reckless water below the weir. A few daring souls have ignored the Restricted sign and have hiked down the slope for a closer look. A prepubescent boy is throwing stones at the pelicans. "Nice," Paula says. "Real nice."

A toddler in pigtails and a Sunday dress joins them, running one sticky hand through Winston's fur. Kailey gives the dog a pat on the head. "Good boy," she says, hopefully. He's been known to snap at children.

"Birdies," the little girl sings, peering through the chain-link fence at the majestic pelicans.

A rakish man jogs up behind her, his legs like twin sticks below the hem of his shorts. "Come on, Amy. Time to go."

The child drops her ice cream cone on the sidewalk and the dogs lap it up. Kailey offers an apologetic smile.

"Why do you think they do it?" Paula asks, leaving the lookout point. They are approaching the parking area near the railway bridge, where people sit in vehicles with their arms hanging out, or walk to the top of the bank to view the rippling water below. The pelicans are most photogenic.

She's lost me, Kailey thinks. "The pelicans?"

"No, them." Paula jerks her head toward a lip-locked couple in a rusted Chev half-ton. The girlfriend's practically sitting in her lover's lap. "I mean, that's the fun part, but as soon as things get serious . . . " Paula whips her index finger across her neck. "Then it's the wedding and guest lists . . . who sits beside who at the reception. Before you know it some old guy with whisky breath is grabbing you in the receiving line and you're expected to kiss him because he's your hubby's great uncle. You want my advice? Skip the 'I dos' and shack up."

Kailey feels the heat creep into her face. She and Mike already have their wedding colours picked out. Their attendants. And they have necked in this same parking lot, back when necking alone was enough.

The dog walkers turn. It's time to double back in the direction they came, this time on the sidewalk. Winston refuses to budge. Kailey picks him up and carries him like a wounded soldier.

"We're conditioned to it," Paula says. "Love. Fail. Love again. It's like a merry-go-round."

"Merry-go-rounds make me sick," Kailey says. She sets Winston on all fours again and shakes out her arms. "But what about true love? The real thing. Do you think it really exists?" The dogs circle each other, sniffing.

"I hope so," Paula offers, but her mouth takes a downward turn, as if she's nibbled one of the liver cakes. "I bloody well hope so."

The animals pull them forward. Paula tells a story: "I had a crazy aunt. Kinda backwards, if my mother was to be believed, but I think she had it together. Said a woman only falls in love once." She changes her voice, does a very bad old lady. "'For me, it was Jimmy Hakle, grade five at the old country school. Even in church he smelled of pigs and the straw stuck to his overalls like glue. Hair like someone had broken a bale on his head. That boy was scabbed all over, but oh, that pink skin underneath.' Who knows?"

Once? Kailey wonders if Mike's the real deal, or if she's wasting her valuable youth on the wrong guy. She scratches her head, pulls out a twig. They reach the crosswalk and wait until there's a break in the traffic, then bolt across Spadina. It's uphill now, toward their homes. Albert cuts Kailey off. Kailey crosses under the leash and yanks her own dog in line. "Wouldn't you once just like to put it all together in words? What you want. What you need."

"Like a personal column?" Paula asks.

"Yeah. Mine would say . . . " she pauses . . . "Wanted: All-round nice guy with big heart and relatively nice feet, by woman with same."

"Go on, do you have a foot fetish?" Paula looks down at her own size nines in the tattered running shoes.

"No. I don't think so. It's just the first thing that came to my mind."

"I don't know how I'd word mine exactly, but I know one thing I'd want. Height. I like tall men. There's nothing worse than having to sacrifice your high heels for a man," Paula says. "I had to hunch in my wedding picture and all through the next two years. It makes my back ache to think of it."

Kailey takes another stab. "I like leather jackets and motorcycles but not bikers. He'd have to cook. Be well travelled. Articulate. Excellent in the sack. Have a good job where there was some kind of danger involved. A cop, maybe. Or a firefighter."

"So *that's* it," Paula says, waiting for Albert to whiz on a tree. "Your definition of the ideal man is someone who puts his life in danger every day?"

"There's always the insurance," Kailey cracks. Paula has taught her well.

They turn right, onto Kailey's avenue. If it were still light out they would have taken their usual route, down the alleys behind the houses on Spadina where they peer through knotholes in fences to glimpse occasional swimming pools and professionally landscaped yards, but tonight it's too late. The sun's retreated into the western horizon. Only a tangerine glow remains.

The dogs are almost obeying now. Six cyclists in jackets with reflective stripes breeze past them, which gets the dogs going again. Winston yips. Albert yaps. They both strain at their leashes.

"Heel!" Kailey and Paula yell together.

"I think we're on the wrong track," Paula says. "Instead of marriage preparation classes, couples should take obedience classes before the big day."

Kailey nods. "At least then we'd know what to expect from each other."

"There'd be tangible rewards . . . " Paula adds.

"Treats!"

"And if anyone got out of hand, the SPCA!"

They dodge a middle-aged man on rollerblades, not knowing who has the right-of-way. Winston growls. "Damn dogs!" the man yells, and rolls right through them.

"No, it wouldn't work," Kailey decides. "The shelter's too full already."

Paula has six pieces of liver cake left. She gives Kailey three. For old times' sake, they go through their dogs' routines.

"Sit."

"Down."

"Stand."

"Roll over." A difficult manoeuvre for the lanky Dalmatian.

"Sit." Again, because it's good practice.

"Speak."

"Get in." To your master's left side and sit.

"Wait." Until you're called.

"Stay." Different than "wait" because the dogs can't move until their masters have walked a few steps away, then returned to their dogs.

"Back." A good one when a dog has muddy feet and wants in the house.

"Let's go."

"Heel."

"Slow."

Paula is teaching her dog a new one. "Give me a kiss, Albert."

"My God," Kailey spurts, "we *are* desperate, aren't we?"

When Kailey's house comes into view they slow down to prolong the night. Even the dogs sense the end is near.

"So, Paula, what's happening behind your mini blinds right now?"

"Oh, he's probably watching TV. No," Paula whips her long hair behind one shoulder, "he *is* watching TV. The sports channel, or some loopy American sitcom. The dinner dishes have crusted over and his laundry's in a sad heap at the bottom of the stairs."

"Newspapers scattered all over the house, dirty gotch on the — " Kailey nips her tongue. If she's presuming too much, Paula doesn't let on. "Why do you think we're so cynical? Sometimes when I see an apparently happy couple, I can't just let them be happy, I have to create problems for them. Maybe her nose is a little too big and it secretly disgusts him . . . "

" . . . or she hates his parents and they're coming to dinner."

The dogs yap at the stars. Paula and Kailey each contemplate their immediate duties. They will water their dogs. Kailey will back-end her reluctant spaniel into his kennel. It's the doghouse for Paula's Dalmatian. He'll whimper until he's too tired.

"Tomorrow night? Same time?" Paula asks, failing to shade her enthusiasm.

"We'll be here," Kailey says. Whatever Mike's got planned, it can wait.

Albert pulls Paula away and Kailey steps inside with Winston. A question blossoms inside her. She scrambles to unlock the door. Paula's already at the end of the block, but she has to know. "Hey! Paula!" she yells from the front yard. "Whatever happened to that clock? You know . . . from the first time around?"

Paula spins and yells back: "I passed it on. A wedding gift for another couple, years ago. I expect it's still out there, somewhere."

"Still ticking?" Kailey questions.

"Like a time bomb."

Toe Jam

Beverley Brenna

I made sure my little brother was sitting on my bed where he couldn't get into trouble. There's no telling what a two year old will do when a guy's busy. Then I started the vacuum. Tanner looked kind of startled at the noise, but he's got to be used to it by now. I mean, I usually have to vacuum on Saturdays, and I'm almost always expected to babysit, too. Even on days like today when I have a cold and would rather be back under the covers planning ways to make money.

I did under the bed first. Balls of dust had multiplied like crazy under there; they don't call them bunnies for nothing. It made me cough just to get close to them. After that I started cleaning the rest of the floor, kicking aside anything in the way.

When I figured I was done, I took one last swipe beside the bed, stepping forward just as I pulled the hose back. That's when it happened. I felt my big toe under the vacuum's power head and in a second my toe was sucked up into the nozzle and twisted around the roller. It felt as though it had been ripped right off.

I swore loudly, forgetting that Tanner was inches away.

"Puck?" he echoed. "PUCK!"

Waves of pain washed over me and the room started to spin. I reached forward and shut off the machine. It didn't help. I was still caught.

Can't pass out, I thought, hanging my head down and taking some deep breaths. Got to think.

I was near a window and maybe someone was out there. I struggled a bit closer, but the vacuum was heavy and the pain increased with every movement.

"Help!" I screamed. "Someone, help me!"

"Puck!" yelled Tanner.

After five minutes of yelling, my voice was hoarse and I was no closer to being saved than a minnow on a sandbar.

Then I heard something. The back door. Mom was home from her early morning run!

"Mom!" I croaked with the voice I had left.

"Puck!" yelled Tanner.

"Hi, boys," she called up the stairs. "I'm just going to go have my shower."

I whimpered. The pain was so bad I felt like puking.

"Go get her," I whispered to Tanner.

He looked at me unsympathetically.

"No way."

"Please," I said hoarsely. "Look, get her and I . . . I'll get you . . . uh . . . french fries. Okay? french fries?"

"Pent pies?"

"Yeah. Get Mom and I'll give you french fries."

He nodded and trotted down the stairs. I closed my eyes and eased myself to a sitting position, the one leg stretched out in front. In a few minutes, I heard the shower start. Then, almost immediately, I heard it stop and Mom yell.

"Leon? Can you take him out of here?"

I reached out and banged on the window with my left hand.

"Leon?"

I banged harder.

Then I heard her coming up the stairs with Tanner.

"Pent pies," Tanner was saying.

"Leon, what — " She saw me and her eyes nearly popped out of her head.

"What's the matter!"

"My toe!" I croaked. "It's in the vac."

"Hold on, I'll pry it open," Mom said, bending down. She gripped the power nozzle and I gave a moan of pain.

"No, don't move it!" I squeaked.

"Pent pies?" Tanner asked.

"Funny, there's no fasteners to undo on the thing," she muttered. "If I could somehow just open it up . . . "

She fiddled with it for a few minutes and I felt like I was inside a dryer with the world whirling by.

"I think I'm going . . . to pass out," I muttered.

"Just a sec," she said. She disappeared, then in a moment put a cold cloth on the back of my neck.

"I do this for sports injuries at school," she said, "when the kid's in shock. Is it helping?"

"Yeah," I said. "But just get me out of this!"

The front door opened and Mom ran into the hall.

"Peter! Come up here!" she called.

"You'll never guess what I got!" he yelled back. "Ferns! Haven't seen them in Superstore for years. Fiddleheads! I bought enough to — "

"Emergency!" Mom bellowed. "Come up here right now!"

"We'll just have to smash the head of the vacuum," said my dad after a quick survey.

"But his toe's in there!" Mom cried.

"Don't move it!" I whimpered.

"And we can't take him to the hospital like this," she went on.

"Pent pies," said Tanner.

"I [illegible] I guess we'll have to call the fire department," Dad said after taking another look. He pulled over the kleenex box from beside the bed and handed me a tissue.

"They'll know what to do!" he comforted.

I blew my nose while Mom went to the phone. In a little while we heard sirens.

"They're here," she cried, flying down to open the door.

Soon these five big firemen, dressed in all their gear, were in my room assessing the situation.

"Are you having any trouble breathing?" the head guy asked, a pencil and clipboard in his hands.

I shook my head, trying to stop my body from shaking.

"He's in a lot of pain," said Dad. "Can you hurry, please?"

"We just need some equipment from the truck," the guy said.

He went back downstairs and a couple of our neighbours pressed their way into the room, and then a couple more. It seemed that, although nobody had heard my cries for help, everybody had seen the fire truck.

I suddenly saw a pile of underwear I'd pushed against the wall. And a few choice magazines left out on the bed. But worst of all, I was wearing my pyjamas. And not just any pyjamas, either. The fish pyjamas. They'd been a birthday gift and I'd planned to wear them for a few days and then lose them. By this time, I was shaking so much that my teeth were chattering.

Just when I thought things couldn't get any worse, they did. I saw her. The new girl from down the street. Her family had moved in about two weeks ago and I'd thought she looked kind of cool. And now here she was, in my bedroom, watching me writhe around on the floor among dirty underwear, my toe in a vacuum cleaner for Pete's sake, wearing these geeky pyjamas. She had on blue overalls, and a necklace of shells hung around her neck. I immediately clenched my teeth together.

The fireman came back and squirted some oily stuff onto the base of my toe. Then one of his partners crouched down with what looked like a miniature jaws of life and in seconds had opened the power head enough to release me.

I could hardly bear to look. Was the toe still attached to my foot? Was it broken? Everyone pushed forward to see. Quickly I put my hand over the toe.

"Can you move it, son?" asked one of the firemen.

"Yeah. It's not . . . not broken," I rasped.

My parents got busy thanking the firemen and filling out forms.

"Show's over," I croaked. People looked disappointed and began to file out. I took a kleenex and wrapped it around the toe. Not that it needed a bandage. It didn't look damaged at all. It wasn't even scraped. Just a bit numb.

"Next time you vacuum, son, wear shoes," said one of the firemen.

"No kidding," I muttered, wishing I were dead. I scrambled to my feet and then quickly sat down on the bed. The room was still acting silly.

"Are you an Aquarius?" asked a voice. I looked up. It was the girl. Her eyes were as green as seaweed.

"Yeah," I answered. "How did you know?"

"I read the horoscopes in the paper this morning. For Aquarius, it said, 'You will get out of a tight squeeze.' It also said your financial situation is unsteady and that you shouldn't make any new business deals."

"Oh," I said. Maybe there was something to these horoscopes after all.

"I'm Summer, by the way."

"Leon."

"Hi." She gave me this big smile. I stared at her and couldn't think of anything more to say. I hoped the part about the unsteady finances wasn't true. I'd just spent money on garlic bulbs to plant in our back garden. Come fall, I planned to make a killing selling garlic to the grocery store.

"I'm a Pisces," she went on. "Neptune enters the most important part of my chart today and I could move from private to reclusive very easily. That's why I have to work on keeping in touch with people. I like your pyjamas, by the way."

"What?"

"Your pyjamas. The fish. That's my sign."

"Oh. Oh yeah," I said. "Pisces, right?"

"Pent pies?" said Tanner hopefully, pulling at my arm.

"He needs his nose wiped," she commented. I looked at him. She was right.

"Must be catching my cold," I said, taking a swipe at his face with the last kleenex in the box.

"See you around," said Summer. "But just not around a vacuum, I guess." She giggled.

"Yeah. See you." I managed a weak smile.

She turned and headed for the door. One of the firemen winked at me. Then he gave me a piece of paper to sign.

"Am I donating my body to science?" I asked.

"Just says that you're satisfactorily rescued," he explained. "Not dead or anything. Are you going to a clinic to have that toe checked out?"

"Nah."

"Fine. You should stay sitting or lying down until the shock symptoms pass. Probably about half an hour should do it," he said.

"Uh-huh. Okay."

"Then it's up and at 'em," he said, winking again. I looked at my pile of underwear and kept quiet.

"That must have been awful," said Mom after she had shown the last of the people out. "I didn't realize vacuums could be so dangerous!"

"I'd better have a look at that toe," said Dad.

"No! It's . . . uh . . . bandaged," I said. "It's pretty shredded, but I think it'll be okay. Eventually."

"You poor thing!" Mom patted my shoulder. "You rest right here and we'll bring whatever you need. Tanner, come along. You mustn't pester your brother now."

"Root beer," I said, "for my sore throat."

"You know," Mom said to Dad on the way downstairs, "our vacuum sure isn't very safe. This was bad, but it could have been worse."

"Yeah," I whispered. "It could have been a lot worse. Like what if I'd been vacuuming naked or something."

They went to the kitchen and I pondered my situation. If I played my cards right, I might get out of all my chores. Maybe I could even con my folks into digging the garlic beds that were going to make me rich. I wiggled my toe. The memory of the pain was so fresh, I could almost believe it was still hurting.

"Oh . . . " I moaned.

"Maybe some ice would help," Mom called.

I smiled. Yes, I had them right where I wanted them. A long Saturday lay ahead. No chores. No babysitting. Then I thought of Summer. Maybe I'd limp over there later, to thank her for coming by. Or . . . maybe I'd wait a few days. See what my horoscope said before rushing into anything.

Flying Toasters

Sharon Stewart

Denny keyed in the remote connection. She found the file she was looking for and clicked on DOWNLOAD. When the screen flashed TRANSFER COMPLETED, she surfed back to her service provider. The file had appeared in her mailbox. She downloaded it to her home machine and ran a standard virus check. The file was clean, so she transferred it into her exec. directory. Now the computer would run it every time she turned it on.

The phone rang. She picked it up, cradling it in her shoulder. It was Mike Franklin, her boyfriend.

"Yo, Mike," she said. "Yeah, I got it. It hasn't run yet. Should come up onscreen any minute now."

Suddenly images appeared. Tiny little gizmos, pink with blue wings, flapped across the screen. They looked kind of like toasters, Denny thought. Some chugged straight ahead, while others flipped over, reversed direction, or crashed into each other.

She chuckled. "Hey, it works," she said into the phone. "Crazy toasters. And there are supposed to be plenty of other images too. I can't wait to see the look on Mom's face. Well, see you tomorrow. Bye."

The toasters were still working fine the next afternoon. Denny saw quite a lot of them, because she was trying to do an English assignment and couldn't think of anything to write. It was funny how she felt kind of happy and peaceful watching the toasters.

Around five, her mother got home from work, having picked up Grub, Denny's little brother, from daycare. She called hello from the hall, then a moment later she appeared, carrying Grub. She put him down, saying, "Would you keep an eye on the monster child while I get changed?" Then she saw the screen. "What on earth are those?" she asked, walking across to stare at the display. Grub toddled after her.

Denny looked up at her, grinning. "New kind of screensaver," she said. "Yo, Grubster," she added as he clambered into her lap.

Grub pointed at the computer screen. "Iss?" he asked.

"Toasters, Grub," said Denny, grinning. "Flying toasters."

"'Oasers," he repeated.

"What will the nerds come up with next?" Her mother shook her head.

Denny shrugged. "Nothing new about screensavers. But this one's supposed to be some big deal upgrade. I had to go all over the Net to find it."

Her mother shook her head. "I don't know how you kids pick up all this stuff."

"Born wired, I guess," said Denny smugly.

"Well, look at that," her mother said, glancing down at Grub. "Usually he's completely wild by this time in the afternoon," she went on. "Eileen at the daycare said he's been tearing the place apart."

After staring blissfully at the screen for a couple of minutes, Grub had gone to sleep with his thumb in his mouth.

"Miracles happen," said Denny, as her mother tiptoed away.

Denny hitched herself closer to the computer, shifting Grub across her lap. She really had to make a start on that essay.

It wasn't until later that she noticed anything odd. She'd left the computer on while she ate supper, and came back to find the toasters on the screen. She settled in and went on with the essay. After an hour, she stopped. Something was distracting her, as if some movement was going on just outside her field of vision. She looked around. Nothing. She started working, and in a moment she had the same sensation again.

Denny looked over her shoulder, and there it was. A tiny toaster. It was flapping slowly through the air just about eye level, but off to one side.

"Whoa!" she muttered, closing her eyes. When she opened them, the toaster was still there. As she watched, another one plinked into existence, and then another.

She stared, open-mouthed, while the toasters bumped into each other and set off in separate directions.

Denny giggled. "Boy, I'm seein' things!" she said. "I'm for bed." She got up and switched off the computer. The toasters vanished.

Well, of course they did, she told herself. They were never there!

She told Mike about it at school the next day. He grinned.

"You're loopy, girl," he told her.

"Guess I was just tired," she admitted.

When she got home, she smelled peanut butter cookies, and followed her nose to the kitchen. Her mother was just removing them from the oven. She was wearing jeans and a sloppy sweatshirt, and her hair was in a messy ponytail.

"Wow!" Denny said, reaching for a cookie. "It's a supermom attack!"

"It happens," said her mother, looking sheepish. "Hey, be careful. Those are still hot." She started putting the cookies on a rack to cool. "I worked at home today," she went on. "Big policy paper for the Minister. I got it all done, and then, oh, I don't know . . . "

"Mothering just sneaked up and ambushed you," finished Denny, juggling the hot cookie. "Hey, no problem. I love it!" She looked around. "Where's Grub?"

"Under the table. He's been some kind of animal all day. A bear, I think," said her mother.

Denny checked under the table. "Excuse me, but he's not here," she reported.

"Oh, lord," wailed her mother. "He's faster than lightning! I left the computer on. If he gets at it, or into my papers . . . "

"I'll find him," said Denny, charging back down the hall.

She didn't have to go far. Grub was sitting on the floor of the den. He beamed at her as she appeared in the doorway. "'Oasers," he said, pointing at the bookcase. Sure enough, a covey of flying toasters was flapping along one of the shelves.

"I don't believe this," Denny muttered. She called back down the hall, "It's okay, Mom." Then she shut the door. If Mom sees this, she'll go ballistic, she told herself, watching the toasters loop the loop in formation.

She hit SAVE, then keyed in the commands to exit the word processing programme. Then she switched the computer off and looked around.

No toasters.

Grub crinkled up his face and got ready to howl.

"Hold on, Grubbie," Denny said, turning the computer on again. After a minute, the toasters reappeared on the screen. Not long after, the first one plinked into view over Grub's head. He chuckled, pleased.

Swell, Denny said to herself. Now what? She reached for the phone. When Mike answered, she said, "You've got to come over. I need to show you something."

"*Now?*" he protested. "It's suppertime, and Mom's making lasagna."

"Forget your stomach," she said. "Tell your mom you're having supper with us. Just get here! Fast!"

Mike sighed. "Okay, okay. Chill out, will you, Denny?"

The intercom buzzed ten minutes later.

"It's okay about dinner," Denny told Mike as she let him into the apartment. "I told Mom we have to work on a project."

"As long as you feed me," he said.

"Here, take this," she replied, stuffing a peanut butter cookie in his mouth. Then she dragged him into the den and shut the door behind them.

"Now, what do you think of that?" she demanded, pointing.

Grub, who had refused to be parted from the toasters, pointed too, grinning.

The air was full of them now.

Mike nearly choked on his cookie. "Mmnf!" he mumbled.

Denny folded her arms. "Is that all you have to say?"

Mike sank down on the computer chair. First he looked at the toasters on the screen, then at the ones in the air.

"I didn't see nearly this many before," Denny told him. "But Mom's had the computer on all day."

"So turn it off," said Mike.

"I tried that, dummy. They just come back when you switch it on again."

"Oh. Well, there's something screwy about this. Better delete the screensaver file from the memory."

They brought the contents of the exec. directory up on screen, but . . .

"It isn't there!" yelped Denny.

"Are you sure this is where you put it?" asked Mike.

"Sure I'm sure. How else would the programme run?" demanded Denny.

"Yeah, well, it's not there now. Let's try FIND FILE," he suggested. "What's the name of it?"

"ScreenTastic," said Denny.

NO FILE FOUND read the screen.

"So much for that," said Michael, scratching his head. "There must be something screwy in the 'ware itself. Didn't you run a virus scan on it?"

"'Course I did!" Denny was indignant. "How dumb do you think I am?"

"Okay, okay. Let me think," he said, sitting back and staring at the screen.

After a minute, the toasters reappeared. Soon Mike and Denny were sitting in the middle of a large swarm of them. Mike waved his hand through them. They seemed to go right through him.

Mike chuckled. "They tickled a bit," he said. "Like a very faint electric shock." He watched the toasters for a few moments, then turned to Denny, grinning. "You know, I kind of like them," he admitted.

"I know what you mean," said Denny. "They make you feel sort of . . . peaceful."

"Why get rid of them, then?"

"Are you kidding?" Denny demanded. "Mom will have a fit if she sees them. She'll get right on my case about messing up her new computer."

"Okay, okay. But let's leave it until after dinner," Mike bargained. "Keep the door closed so your mom doesn't see them."

Denny nodded and picked up Grub. "More toasters later," she promised him. "After supper."

"'Oasers funny," Grub chortled.

"You bet," Mike agreed, switching the light off and closing the door behind them.

The toasters had disappeared when they got back after supper. Instead, raindrops were falling soundlessly on the computer screen and slanting through the room.

"What's this?" demanded Mike.

Denny slammed the door shut and leaned against it. "I bet it's Pitter Patter."

"Huh?"

"There were other settings besides the toasters. Pitter Patter. Bouncing Nerds. Who knows what else?"

"You mean this thing is resetting itself, as well as running around inside the drive?"

Denny nodded. "Looks like it."

Mike slumped down in the computer chair and scowled at the screen. Pitter-pats of electronic rain beat down on him. After a couple of minutes he stopped scowling and stretched. "Jeez, I feel so relaxed," he said, yawning. "No use getting ourselves all worked up about it. What harm is it doing?"

Denny dragged him out of the chair. "Get away from that screen. I've already got one addict in the family. Grub and his 'oasers. Not you too!" She pushed him into the hall and closed the door behind them.

After a moment, he blinked, and said, "Yeah, I guess we'd better do something. But it's way beyond me. There's only one guy who might know what to do."

Denny gasped. "You mean . . . "

"Yeah. Meganerd."

"Oh, come on, Mike. Alex Bates won't talk to us. He thinks we're cretins."

"Well, compared to him we *are* cretins," said Mike, picking up the hall phone and dialling. "Yo, Alex?" he said a moment later. "It's Mike Franklin. Yeah, I know you're busy, so I'll give it to you quick. Heard anything about that hot new screensaver program out of HSL Labs? Yeah, Denny and I did, too. Well, she downloaded it. And guess what? We've got virtual flying toasters."

Leaning over his shoulder, Denny heard a muffled squawk.

"Yep, virtual," Mike went on. "Swarms of them flying around the room. Not to mention electronic raindrops falling on our heads."

Squawk, squawk went the phone.

"Yeah, we tried all that. The darn thing has exited the exec. directory. We can't find it. And it's resetting itself. Yeah. Must be some weird virus."

Denny grabbed the receiver. "Alex? Denny. Listen, you gotta help us. My mom will ground me for life if she finds out I've screwed up her new computer."

"Uh, hi, Denny," said Alex. "Okay. Lemme think." There was a moment's silence, then he went on, "Your virus disinfectant's probably out of date. I know a guy at U Chicago who's up on all the latest weird stuff out there. Let me see if I can download something from him and put it on a disk. Shouldn't take long."

"We'll come pick it up," offered Denny.

"Nah, I'll bring it over," Alex said. "Virtual toasters I gotta see!"

"Well, if you're like everyone else around here, you'll love 'em," said Denny, and hung up. "Gee," she said to Mike. "He's actually coming over."

Mike shrugged. "Well, natch. It's something to do with computers."

The buzzer went off forty minutes later.

"I'll get it, Mom," yelled Denny, heading for the intercom. "Just someone else who's working on the project."

Her mother peered at her over the back of the couch. "Another one? How many does it take?"

Alex looked as if he hadn't slept for a week. His hair was uncombed, and his glasses needed cleaning. "Here y'are," he said, holding out a disk. "Now, show me."

"In there," said Denny, pointing him toward the den.

They found Mike in front of the computer again, peacefully watching electronic raindrops falling on the screen. They were all around him, too.

"Way cool," said Alex, waving his hand through the image field.

"Yo, Meganerd," said Mike grinning. "Howza boy?"

Alex turned to Denny. "Is Franklin on something?"

"They kind of make you feel good," Denny ventured. "Sort of relaxed. My little brother absolutely loves them. The flying toasters, that is."

"Hmmm." Alex looked thoughtful. His glasses had slid down his nose, and he pushed them up with one finger. "Well, let's see what this disinfectant will do," he said. Then, "Move your butt, Franklin," he added, yanking the chair out from under him.

He hitched it closer to the computer and put the disk in the disk drive. His fingers danced over the keys as he saved it into the exec. directory and then ran it.

"Chicago guy says this should kill off just about any known Trojan horses and viruses," he said over his shoulder. "Of course, it's all through your computer now."

"Swell," groaned Denny, trying to calculate how many years of her allowance it would take to buy her mother a new computer.

NO VIRUSES DETECTED read the screen.

"Oh, yeah?" said Mike, grinning.

"I'll try RESET," said Alex, hitting another command.

The onscreen images died, and the raindrops disappeared from the air.

Denny cheered as the screen returned to normal. A minute later, she fell silent as the screen filled with images again. This time it was weird little guys on pogo sticks.

Mike snickered. "Bouncing Nerds, I presume," he said.

Pretty soon the air was full of them. Denny shot a glance at Alex. His mouth was curling a bit at one corner. Meganerd was actually trying to smile!

Great, she said to herself. They've got to him too! She herself was finding it hard to keep worrying about the images. They were harmless, weren't they? In a way, they were pretty funny.

"Well, folks, it's not a virus. At least not a virus known to man," said Alex. He glanced at Denny. "I mean, to persons," he added.

"So what do we do now?" Mike wanted to know.

"Keep it, of course. Study it," said Alex.

"Not on my mom's computer, you don't," protested Denny.

"You can always download the thing from the remote site if you want to play around with it," Mike reminded Alex.

"True," said Alex. He leaned back in the chair. "Well, we can't find it, or disinfect it," he replied. "Only way to get rid of it would be to wipe the computer's hard drive."

"You mean, wipe the entire memory?" asked Denny, horrified. "My mom would skin me alive!"

"And if you leave it the way it is?" Alex asked, peering at her through his cloudy glasses.

Denny swallowed hard. "Same thing," she admitted.

"So?" he prodded.

"I guess we'd better get rid of it," she whispered.

"Yeah, but how?" Mike cut in. "What do we do? Nuke the computer?"

Alex winced. "Does your mom have the disks for the operating system and all the other 'ware that's on the drive?" he asked, turning to Denny.

"Yeah, I think so." Denny pointed to a pile of boxes on one of the shelves.

Alex went over and flipped through them quickly. "Yep, looks like everything's here. It can all be reinstalled once the drive is clear." He selected a floppy disk and inserted it into the drive. Then he pressed a couple of keys and sat back, waiting.

Moments later, the Bouncing Nerds disappeared from the air and the screen went blank blue.

"Wow," said Denny.

"That's it?" Mike asked.

Alex nodded. "It's a wipe," he said. "I rebooted off a system floppy and reformatted the hard drive. That'll wipe out everything that's on it. Goodbye, virus."

"You're *sure*?" asked Denny.

"Sure I'm sure. Of course, your mom will have to reinstall all the other software from her purchase disks, if she's into that kind of thing. Or you can get the dealer to do it."

Mike whooped, and the three of them exchanged high fives.

"Now don't go downloading any more wild-eyed 'ware," said Alex, from the doorway. He winked at Denny and closed the door behind him.

"He's not such a bad guy after all," said Denny.

"The Bouncing Nerds musta got to him," said Mike.

The next morning, Denny's mother was running late. "I've got to look really together today," she fretted, as she dashed around the kitchen. "My Minister wants me to brief the Prime Minister about the policy paper I just did."

"Want me to finish feeding Grub?" Denny offered.

"Would you? Thanks!"

"C'mon, Grubbo. Open wide," Denny said, prodding his lips with a spoonful of cereal.

He didn't seem much interested in his breakfast. In fact, he kept looking around the room as if he expected to see something.

"'Oasers?" he asked hopefully.

"No more toasters," Denny said firmly, taking the opportunity to pop the spoon into his open mouth. "Ever."

After school, Denny switched on the computer. The screen was still blank blue. She put in a call to the computer service company to reinstall the computer's software.

"What do you mean the hard disk has been wiped?" the guy on the phone wanted to know. "What stupid jerk did that?"

"Who knows?" said Denny, crossing her fingers behind her back. "Anyway, we have all the disks. But we'd sorta rather someone else did the reinstalling."

"Okay, okay," he grumbled. "I'll send somebody out."

Denny wandered into the living room and turned on the TV. It was tuned to Newsworld, and she was about to switch it off when she realized the House of Commons Question Period was being broadcast live.

I wonder if they're talking about Mom's policy stuff, she thought, perching on the edge of the couch. She tried to follow the debate, but all she could figure out was that the Leader of the Opposition was all worked up about something.

He kept yelling and pointing his finger at the Prime Minister.

She heard her mother's key in the lock and went out to meet her. "Hi. How did your big deal policy thing go?" she asked, collecting Grub and skinning him out of his jacket.

Her mother beamed. "Great. Just great," she said. "My minister was really pleased at the way I briefed the PM. He's using some of the stuff I did in the House this afternoon."

Figuring this was a good moment, Denny said, "Uh, Mom? The computer's gone weird. I called the company and they're sending a service guy over."

Her mother groaned. "Oh, for heaven's sake. The darn thing's brand new!"

Denny went back to the living room, where Grub was sitting in front of the TV set. She looked around for the remote to change the channel.

"Pretty boring stuff, Grubster?" she asked. "How about a touch of Barney?"

He grinned up at her. "'Oasers," he announced.

"Huh?" Denny whirled and scanned every corner of the room. "You're goofy, Grub. There aren't any toasters here."

He nodded and pointed at the TV screen. "'Oasers," he insisted.

Then she saw them. A covey of toasters flapped past the end of the Prime Minister's nose. He blinked, and waved his hand in front of his face.

"Excuse me, Mr. Speaker. As I was saying . . . " He started to go on, then stopped again as more toasters plinked into view around him.

Now the Leader of the Opposition was getting to his feet. "Mr. Speaker, I protest. If this government thinks it can distract the Opposition by cheap tricks . . . " He fell silent as more and more toasters began to appear.

"Holy cow!" gasped Denny.

Then the picture disappeared from the screen for a moment. "We are experiencing temporary difficulties with our transmission," a voice announced. "Please do not adjust your set."

There was a babble of voices in the background, but she couldn't hear anything clearly.

Denny grabbed the phone and dialled. "Mike?" she said. "Turn on Newsworld. Never mind why, just do it! And tell Alex!"

She slammed down the receiver just as the picture came back on. The camera scanned the House of Commons, showing flights of toasters looping and tacking through the air. The Members of Parliament had poured down onto the floor. Some looked dazed. Others were batting at the toasters. The Prime Minister and the Leader of the Opposition were standing together in the middle of the floor of the House. Oddly enough, both were grinning.

"Crazy toasters! They're getting to them, too," muttered Denny. "But how did they get there? It couldn't be . . . "

Her mother came into the room. "How's the PM's speech going?" she asked. Then she stopped dead and stared at the screen. "Whaaa . . . ?" she gasped.

Denny was thinking furiously. "Mom?" she said, after a minute. "That stuff you worked on. Did you print it out?"

"Of course not," her mother replied. "I saved it on the hard drive as I worked. When it was finished, I put it on a floppy disk and took it to work with me."

A disk! Her mother must have copied the virus onto the disk along with her report! And then . . .

"Did . . . did you give the disk to anyone?" she asked, afraid she knew the answer already.

"Sure," said her mother, still absorbed in the toasters. "I put it into my computer at work and e-mailed an attached file to everyone at the ministry. I even gave a copy of the disk to the PM. He was going to input it into his laptop, he said."

And guess who used his laptop in the House this afternoon? Denny finished to herself. Oh, lordy!

She scrunched down into the couch cushions, her eyes glued on the screen. Some of the MPs were laughing together and slapping each other on the back. Others were just watching the toasters with blissed-out expressions on their faces.

"Those toasters. Aren't they like the ones on your new screensaver?" her mother asked.

"Uh-huh," said Denny. Her mind was racing. The guy who invented the software intended this to happen! she thought. He put the virus there on purpose! He knows what the images do to people!

And all over the world people like her were probably downloading the programme through the Internet and spreading it around. And everywhere there was a computer . . .

Lots of things had computers, didn't they? Not just governments and businesses. Armies and navies. And all their warplanes and ships and tanks.

Denny swallowed hard.

Her mother was smiling now, as she watched the antics of the toasters. "This is crazy, isn't it?" she said, turning to Denny. "What on earth is happening?"

"I think peace just broke out," said Denny in a small voice.

She just hoped nobody would blame it on *her*!

THE TROG KING AND THE FOOL

JENNIFER TAYLOR

"You are such a fool, Jason Whitmore." Delia Roberts walked away, leaving Jason juggling her apple and two oranges.

"Don't you want your apple back?"

"After your grubby hands have been all over it? No thanks."

"How about an orange?"

She didn't even bother to answer and Jason felt his chest tighten. He had spent all summer practising his juggling just to impress Delia, and this was it?

"Hey, Whitmore! Can you juggle four?" Someone from the football team tossed a second apple at him, and Jason scooped it effortlessly into his sequence.

"Not bad, Witless. How about five?" Another orange flew at him and he grabbed for it.

Sweat began to bead on his brow now that the entire cafeteria was watching. Trust the football trogs to demand a show when Delia had already left the room.

Troglodyte was Jason's favourite word. It perfectly described the cave-dwelling morons who would rather toss a pigskin or fruit around the cafeteria than ever open a book. The trogs were getting restless and Jason's arms were getting tired.

"Hey, calendar boy. Catch!"

Jason didn't have time to regret the day he had loudly announced you could spell his name July, August, September, October, November, as a banana peel came flying at his head.

Staggering back, still swirling the rest of the fruit, he crashed into a bench. A shower of apples and oranges poured down on his head as pain washed over him.

"Excellent, Fool. Get up now."

Jason forced his eyes open and found himself staring into the blurry faces of the football team. Before he could wonder why they were half dressed in their gear, the trogs hauled him to his feet and sent him spiralling into the centre of the room. They let out a great cheer as he collided with a large chair.

Slumped at its base Jason lay still, puzzled that the trogs were wearing old fashioned leather shoulder pads. And a few had chain mail vests that glittered in the torchlight. Chain mail? Torchlight? Jason rubbed his head and groaned.

"Are you well, Fool?"

"My head hurts and my arm."

"As do mine on days like this." The old man in the crown nodded and touched his brow. "The arm of justice often aches with the decision of the crown. But come now, walk with me."

Despite his confusion, Jason struggled to his feet and followed the man. The trogs roared their delight as Jason almost tripped over a sleeping dog, but he managed to escape the hall intact.

"Are you a king?"

The old man stopped. "You are good to remind me of my place, Fool. A king is still only a man. I fear this evening will test us both. The enemy awaits."

Jason's step faltered. Things were getting a little too weird and the word "enemy" was not reassuring. Maybe he had wandered out of the cafeteria and into a special history project, Medieval Reconstruction or something. Before he could ask, the King disappeared through a dark wooden doorway and Jason hurried after him.

They both slowed as they entered a cavernous room. Stripped of all furniture except two chairs by the fireplace, the empty space was still filled with the presence of the man pacing before the fire. The enemy was the biggest trog Jason had ever seen.

"Enough waiting. My men may be enjoying your feast but I demand your decision."

"Sit, friend, and we will talk." The King motioned for the angry man to join him at the fireside. "Play something, Fool."

Play? Jason froze. Play what? Music? He doubted either man shared his taste in classic rock. Anyway there was no CD player in sight. His gaze fell on the sword at the Trog King's side: the shiny, sharp, pointy sword hidden in its leather scabbard.

Jason gave an involuntary hop away from the two kings and almost somersaulted over a lute. He grasped the instrument and wondered how much it was like a guitar. Not that he played the guitar very well. Why hadn't he practised more?

"Would you like me to juggle?" he offered.

The old king gave a slight shake of his head and Jason plunked himself down and began to pluck strings. Would they recognize "Stairway to Heaven" played badly on a lute? Struggling to remember the notes, Jason began to relax with the familiar rhythm of the song. The kings ignored him and set to talking.

Coming to the end of the tune for the second time Jason's fingers froze in a tangle of notes as a girl walked into the room. Delia! He jumped up in surprise but she ignored him, which was no surprise.

"You sent for me, Father." She spoke formally and stood stiffly by the king's side.

Jason's confusion set his head pounding.

"Yes, Cordelia. In exchange for peace, our new friend and ally has agreed to marry you." He reached out and put her hand in the Trog King's.

"No!" Jason's shout startled everyone including himself.

The Trog King thrust Cordelia away and drew his sword. "You challenge me, Fool?"

Jason stood his ground trying not to shake. "You can't barter people's affections." He swallowed hard as the Trog King advanced toward him. "Don't you want to marry someone for love?"

"Love?" The Trog King turned to Delia. "Do you love me?"

She grew pale but slowly shook her head.

"Then it's a good thing I love to fight." The Trog King spun around to face Jason who gripped the neck of the lute like a baseball bat.

"Your choice of weapons is a lute?" The Trog King's question became a menacing growl as he splintered the instrument into several pieces with one slice of his sword. The growl became a laugh as the Trog King sheathed the blade.

"A most wise Fool, I feel much better now." He turned back to the King and Delia. "Although I see I have lost a bride, I will honour our pact for your daughter's weight in gold."

Jason was stunned into silence. His arm reverberated from the shock of the sword blow and his wrist felt shattered. Dragging his gaze away from the scattered pieces of the lute, he saw Delia smile. His sense of triumph faded with the Trog King's next words.

"The gold and your fool in exchange for peace. Let us shake hands in agreement."

Jason didn't want to hear any more. He would have run away but his hand was engulfed in the Trog King's meaty clasp. A wave of pain sent Jason crumpling to the floor.

"Jason. Can you hear us?" The voice was calm and reassuring, and saying his name. He was so relieved he wanted to leap up but strong hands held him back.

"Lie still. You've had a bad fall and hurt your head."

His head? Now that they mentioned it, it hurt worse than anything he had ever felt. No, he corrected himself, it didn't hurt as much as his hand. When he tried to move it he almost blacked out.

"You've probably broken your wrist too. Your parents are coming to take you for X-rays at the hospital."

Jason roused himself enough to look around. The room was bright, sunny and very modern. Somewhere a telephone rang followed by a bell for class change. School. He closed his eyes in relief.

"Can I see him, please?"

Jason's heart began to pound as he recognized Delia's voice. He forced himself to sit up, then wished he hadn't as the room began to spin.

"Jason? You look awful."

Through a haze of pain, Jason managed a whisper. "Delia?"

"I'm right here."

"Promise me you won't marry the Trog King."

"Is a Trog King like a Frog Prince? I think I can safely promise you I don't intend to marry either one. I just came to tell you I can drop off any homework or books you need at home. Guess you won't be juggling for a while."

"But will I be able to play the guitar?"

"I didn't know you played it."

"Not very well."

"Well, if you get good enough you can give me a private concert."

The second bell rang and Delia said goodbye. Jason was already planning his song list. As soon as his cast was off he would practise until he was ready. Then he would give Delia her concert in a cosy room with a fireplace — and no trogs in sight.

Dragon's Breath

Karen Krossing

We called ourselves the gore gang — Tara, Carter, and me. Tara looking like a giant lump of clay moulded into a mutant mud monster — but with a wicked mind. Carter with giant fish eyes and a knack for getting under your skin whenever he opened his mouth. And me, Nealon — a body patterned after useless bits of wire with a serious computer chip for a brain.

"Okay, we all know the game," I began. "But for those whose memory slots are jammed, I'll give you a kick-start." I ogled at Carter as I said the last part, but he didn't twig that I was talking about him.

"The rules are no swearing and no repeating what's been said before. You gotta stay on topic, and be creative but as gory as possible. Did you hear that, Carter?" I said in a louder voice to show him that his tedious existence on this earth was a waste of my time. "Creative, yet gory. We want stories about deformed hunks of flesh hanging off semi-human frames. Kneecaps swinging backwards and noses turned inside out."

"Quit singing your song, and let's crank the gears," urged Carter. But Tara only watched me through large brown eyes like she could see into my soul.

"It's my turn to pick the topic," I continued, pleased with my own sense of control and wit, "and I've got a good one. Are you ready?"

Daisy, cuddled into a pink blanket beside me, murmured in her sleep as if in answer. I never babysat anymore, except for her. Daisy, the four year old who ducked her head to go under bridges. Who was sure that, one day, she would grow up to be older than I was. I could never peg her. She was like that spot in the middle of the sun that you can never really see, even if you squint.

I leaned towards Tara and Carter and whispered intimately, "Tonight's topic is metal meets meat." I'd had visions of computer-controlled spaceships gracefully crushing humanoids. Fantasies of cyberprobes fusing with brain matter. I knew I could win this one. After all, Nealon means champion, and I was sure that I could live up to my name.

"Let the games begin," I announced. We faced off — Carter and Tara on one couch, Daisy and me on the other, and a pile of candied junk on the coffee table between us. We'd been gorging for the last hour on sweets and treats from Tara's father's candy shop, waiting for Daisy to fall asleep. You see, I had a deal with Daisy — she didn't tell her parents that I let the gang come over and I let her stay up until her parents came home.

We always started gore talk by trying to get each other to flinch through the sheer blood and guts of our words. We scored when we made someone react. But the real way to tell the winner was by seeing who was left talking at the end. It was sort of like a gunfight from an old western. Sometimes Tara would say nothing until the very end, then come out with one deadly line that was enough to flatten us.

You might be wondering why we did this. Why try to gross each other out? You see, most people we knew treated words like tools. They used techno-speak or even empty curses, but their words had lost their power, their soul. The only thing left for us was gore — pure, offensive, physical carnage. We wanted to return the lifeblood to the way we talked. We wanted to fling contempt at whatever enslaved us. Together, we sent out a battle cry against the enemy — the adult world of authority and conformity.

But what actually was to happen that night, accidentally or not, is that we returned the power of enchantment to our words. We stumbled upon something unexpected — a language with its own colour, passion, and magic.

"I got one," started Carter. "Picture this. Spock screamed as the alien ship collided with the shuttlecraft. The ship crushed his body against the walls of the shuttlecraft like a sardine in a can."

I got a little fired up at Carter right away because he stole my idea, but he said it first so I couldn't complain. Anyway, if I'd said it I wouldn't have needed to use *Star Trek* — I had my own ideas.

Tara followed Carter with, "A sharp knife tearing through his scalp. Pain searing his nerve endings. She raised it above her head like a victory token. The enemy conquered." Tara talked slowly, with a sort of a drawl. And her delivery was always timed perfectly.

Carter and I rolled our eyes, careful not to react too much. But she had scored big.

I went next. "He hooks the cyberprobes into his temple implants, but the system's been fixed. Snap. Crackle. Pop. The prongs in his head fuse with his brain matter."

Tara was cool, but Carter had broken down with that one — he was cracking his knuckles. I could tell that he wished he'd said it.

Carter countered my take with, "Half-dead, corpse-like zombie bashing against the inside of the coffin until the broken bones point through mangled flesh." Carter hardly cared what he said. He always tried to get in as many quips as he could.

"Since when are coffins made of metal?" I asked coolly. Tara nodded. Carter, red in the face, knew he was falling behind.

"The bullet pierced his chest and exploded through the other side," I said, then paused for a moment in anticipation of the punch line. "Lead poisoning." Tara laughed, which was a score for me. I was out in front.

Then she hit us with a killer. "Kitchen table, no anesthetic. Doctor saws through the skull with rusty metal tackle, then fumbles with the scrambled brains." I could have cried — it caught me in the throat. But I held myself together, although Carter whimpered like a dog.

I had to stay in the race. So I cast off with, "And he thought it was bad when the barber gave him a serious case of razor burn! He pressed himself deep into the chair, shrinking from the gleam of the razor as it neared his eye."

Carter rubbed his big fish eyes defensively and I smiled to show my victory. But Tara didn't flinch. She countered with, "Whipping through the ocean air like an arrow of death, the harpoon found its target. Water frothing with blood, the whale thrashed uselessly, stunned by the grisly attack."

As far as I was concerned, Tara and I were tied and Carter had only one score. But Carter wanted back into the game. He said, "The axe smashed into her head until his anger faded. His arms crimson, his face twisted with hate. She would two-time him no more."

"Bloody wife-beater," exploded Tara. Then she caught herself, but it was too late. Carter had hit her where he knew she'd hurt.

I took the chance to make a move. "After the bomb," I began, making it up as I went along, "massive techno-bugs fitted with killer metal jaws hunted down the few humans that had survived."

I thought I did well, but Tara's earthy face showed her determination. "Meat slapped onto the cutting board," she called out. "Butcher's knife flashing silver. The soul of the dead cow crying out."

But she didn't stop there, although Carter started chewing his fingernails and giggling hopelessly. "Needles puncturing sickly arms riddled with past tracks. Total anguish until the juice brings a false release."

I tried to get in a word, but she finished with: "Jamming the tip of the pen through his hand again and again until it was only an offensive stub, he had written his last corny love poem."

A triple whammy. I stared at her with renewed respect. I could think of nothing to say.

Then Carter found himself. "He broke through the guts of the worms with his fingers, piercing it with the hook as metal meets meat. 'Fish food,' he muttered as he tossed it into the water."

"Hey," I exploded, although his effort was lame. "Renege. Can't say 'metal meets meat.' It's been used." I glanced at Tara for support, but she was shaking her head.

"No way, Nealon," she said. "The topic's not part of the game. Can be used once. Carter scores. You reacted."

I was shaking with fury, but I didn't dare argue because I didn't want to give him a bigger score. I'd bowed to Tara's skill, but I figured I was still ahead of Carter. But the way I felt about him I could've flushed him down the toilet like some dead guppy.

But Carter wasn't finished with me yet. "Can't take it, huh, Nealon? Can always tell when you're nervous. You yank at the bum-fluff growing on your chin like you think if you pull it out it'll make you a man."

Now I know I've got some bad personal habits, but at least I'm smart. I'm going to be either a radio announcer or a geneticist. But Carter was hitting low. I jerked my hand away from the few hairs that were growing on my chin and focussed my rage on him.

"You want to talk about metal meets meat! I'll give it to you. I'll slam into your fish face with a bunch of fives studded with diamond rings. I'll gouge those watery fish eyes out of your face with dull spoons. I'll strangle you with metal wires until you ooze eyeball soup." I was on a roll.

"I don't have to listen to this," spouted Carter. "I'm going to get rid of the bladder matter." He stood up to leave and I was satisfied.

But then Tara said, "You're foul, Nealon. Week-old underwear stained with skid marks hanging off the carphone antennae. This is a battle of wits, not insults and toilet talk."

I heard Carter giggling horribly from the hallway. "You want to see something funny?" I asked him. "Get a load of mama palooka." I gestured towards Tara. "You'd think it was someone's idea of a crazy joke to see her trying to fit into one of those chairs at school with the little desks attached. She thinks she's so smart — just wait until the day her brain overloads. Bam. Putrid cow flesh everywhere."

My talk became a frenzy of yak. Hurling insults with each breath, I couldn't hear anyone else and I couldn't stop using Tara and Carter for target practice. I'd grabbed the moment by the throat and I had to follow it home. That's why it took me a minute to realize that those wild noises weren't coming from me, but from Daisy beside me.

While I was still shooting hot air, Daisy had begun to burble nonsense like she'd swallowed the dictionary. She was still in that place between waking and sleep when I finally halted my own shattering noise. She rocked and sang in a sort of rhythmic chant that grew louder and louder. Suddenly, she stood up, shrieking a long string of words that I couldn't get my head around. With her hands gesturing like wands, she stared at me with blue, china-doll eyes. Her face was deadpan.

"Shut up, dragon's breath!" she screamed out at me from a place deep inside her. Then silence, except for the gong of the clock on the mantel as it struck midnight.

Her white skin was paler than I'd ever seen and her wispy blonde hair was damp with sweat. The first thing I thought was, "For a kid, that was pretty good talk."

I knew I had to say something — a comeback of some sort — but I couldn't think of anything. Tara and Carter were just waiting for me to react like they were watching some TV show. I opened my mouth, but only a tiny puff of smoke came out. In a daze, I let out a gut-wrenching roar of protest, but I was as shocked as the others to see a great belch of fire emerge from my mouth and ignite the curtains.

Chaos erupted. Daisy clutched her hands over her mouth, afraid to utter another word. Tara and Carter started smacking the curtains with the pillows from the couch. And I sat still in silent panic, screaming inside my head.

Once the curtains were only smouldering, I began to think about what'd happened. I wasn't really miffed at Daisy. Maybe it wasn't so bad. In a way, it was sort of a gift really. Just think of the people I could intimidate with fire. No one would ever think of me as a featherweight again. I tried to tell Tara and Carter about it — how I'd make yellowbellies out of our enemies. But I couldn't talk. I mean, I couldn't physically say a word.

I wanted to screech, "Help. Can't talk." This was a real blow — I thrived by my wit. I loved the sound of my own voice. I flung desperate glances at my friends and the miniature figure of Daisy, still holding her hands over her mouth.

Tara seemed to understand my case. "Be obscene and not heard," she stated flatly.

I could've whacked her for that one. Did she think this was still the game? Daisy had put some sort of curse on me. Speak no evil. It was no joke. I'd been lashing out with everything I'd had, trying to hurt everyone. But Daisy's words had unleashed a power. Why? How?

Daisy was still a child, and a strange one. Her eyes didn't yet see like an adult's. That's why I liked babysitting her — her world was primitive, but real. Daisy had thrown a curse at me for protection — called upon supernatural powers to effect a change. And the power unleashed by her words was not in the words themselves but in their hidden magical meanings and in the faith of the one who used them.

"Nasty," said Carter as he and Tara came to gawk at me. Daisy huddled sobbing against me, afraid to speak or even look at anyone. I figured we had about one hour until her parents came home. We had to find a way to undo the deed.

Daisy was no help and Carter thought that maybe they should just leave me the way I was. He wanted to finish the game. With a whine caught up in his bugle nose, he fried my eardrums. "I was winning. You're just trying to get out of it," he accused me.

I wanted to whip him with my tongue, except that I'd been silenced. We'd cleaned him out, or at least Tara had, and he was in the hole. But I had a new weapon. I puffed up my scrawny body, trying to look like a rabid dragon, and put my face in his. I gave him my best beg-for-your-life look and thought hard about how good it would be to burn his butt.

But Carter only said, "Whew! What've you been eating, jungle mouth?"

I let out just enough fire to singe his eyebrows — I wanted to torture him slowly.

Carter yelped, then Tara stepped in, forcing us apart. "Sit down, maggot-monger," she ordered Carter. "Are you chasing death?" Then she directed at me, "And you, turn off the fireworks. We gotta do some brain-work."

So Tara and Carter started banging around what to do about me, and I sort of listened. But then, I hit on a new space. With my tongue silenced by fire, I found forgotten noises around me — the ticking of the clock, the rise and fall of the desperate voices of my friends, the soft, quick breathing of Daisy.

I felt connected — like my jarring noise had distracted me from something essential. Only in silence could I hear the footsteps of insight.

But Tara interrupted my revelations. "Got the plan," she announced. "Cooked up a recipe to clear the curse."

She wrote on a piece of paper, *Reverse the curse. Free the Speech.* Then she soaked it in water to dissolve it. And I was to drink it. Simple.

"Water softens the words, making them easier to ingest. They'll become part of you, even if you don't believe. Read about it in a book once," she explained with a shrug of her oversized shoulders. "Moist magic. Palatable to the imagination."

"Better with him clammed up," mumbled Carter. But I snarled at him, and he choked pretty fast.

I wasn't sure what to think about Tara's brew, but I drank it down, gagging a little on the wad of soggy paper. Tara's eyes were on me, and even Carter showed some interest. After waiting a few minutes for the magic to cook, I carefully opened my mouth.

"Champion," I tried to whisper so I wouldn't burn anything, but again there was only smoke.

I glanced down at Daisy for some kind of signal. She tossed her angel head up at me, and for a second, I thought I caught a glimpse of myself in her round-saucer eyes. What must she think of me — to curse me like that? A pizza-faced kid with crooked glasses and a crooked smile. An arrogant kid who thought he could shovel talk like the wind. A kid who could dish the dirt but couldn't take it.

Somehow, Daisy made me feel that adulthood wasn't something I was growing into but that childhood was something that I was forgetting. I felt like I'd fallen out of something — childhood, a way of viewing the world? I couldn't quite catch the concept. But suddenly I wanted to tell Tara that I hadn't meant what I said about her. But Carter . . . well, he was a different story.

Then we heard the rattling of keys in the front door. On cue, Tara and Carter dove for the back door — the game, and me, forgotten. Daisy rushed down the hall to her bed. And I was left to face the music. How did the curtains get burnt? Why won't you speak to us? Maybe I'd set them on fire.

But just as the door was about to open, Daisy's tiny head emerged from her doorway. She walked slowly down the hall towards me, risking trouble.

I wanted to holler, "Get to bed," like a mother or father would. But I couldn't.

Daisy stopped just in front of me and said solemnly, "I take it back." Just like that. Then her parents opened the door and saw her standing there.

"Daisy, what are you still doing up?" shrieked her mother as she bundled Daisy inside her shining black fur coat.

Both her parents glared at me. "I demand an explanation," ordered her father.

I choked and stuttered, not wanting to set them on fire now. But the cards were laid and I had to play. "Guess this is my last babysitting gig here," I said, without even a trace of smoke. Then I winked at Daisy and grabbed my coat. I was going to miss her.

Wishing on the Mouse

Cheryl Archer

Mom made the big announcement at the dinner table back in December, just as I was scrubbing ketchup off my plate with my last french fry.

My little brother Tyler, Dad, and I stared as Mom said she'd discovered the Internet. You could tell she was excited as a three year old at Christmas the way her eyes glittered.

Big deal, I'd thought immediately. Like who doesn't know about the Internet. But there was something about my mother's eyes, the way she looked at us one by one and the way she held her back straight, that kept me from saying anything.

"I've met someone on the Internet," she was saying, quiet as a kiss, "a kindred spirit."

My dad's face turned blood red. "Marge — what are you saying?"

"I'm going away. To meet this person." Her eyes shifted from us. "Tomorrow. I leave tomorrow."

Everyone was quiet. You could've heard a snowflake melt.

Then Tyler does the usual. "Huh? What'd you say?"

I'd swear the kid's deaf. Mom says it's 'cause he's got kissing tonsils. His tonsils are so huge they practically touch together. As if they're kissing. She says it affects his ear canals and that's why he hears so bad.

Dad says Tyler has the tonsils that ate New York. He used to joke like that before Mom left.

I was suddenly wishing I had kissing tonsils.

Anyway, Mom didn't repeat herself. Not to Tyler. Or anyone else.

That was it. No discussion. No further explanations. Not even a goodbye.

When I woke up the next morning she was gone.

It's been three weeks now and my dad still won't talk about it. Just runs his large hands through his hair, what's left of it anyway, and says it's none of my business.

Like heck. What am I supposed to do? Pretend nothing's wrong? What if something awful happened? Like some weird Internet maniac has her locked up somewhere. Terrible thoughts crash around until my head feels like a pinball machine. It's driving me crazy.

Maybe my dad figures if he doesn't say anything and we pretend nothing's happened, she'll just show up one day and everything'll be the same. I noticed he's still wearing his gold wedding band. The engraving on the inside says: *Yours forever. Love M.*

Forever. Whatever that means. She hasn't even called.

Suddenly snow's hitting me in the legs and I remember what I'm supposed to be doing. It's the reason I'm standing here with snow up to my kneecaps, wearing ten layers of clothing and holding a cut-up antifreeze bottle. Why else would anyone be outside when it's twenty-five below with a 1500 windchill? When it's so cold your face could freeze off in less than a minute?

My teacher, Mr. Fancy, is waving his shiny aluminum shovel at me from the other side of the clearing. He's hollering to get working, to get digging.

There's snow blasting out the doorway of our *quinzhee*— the Inuit word for the snow shelter we're building. The snow's flying in all directions. It's like a blizzard happening in front of me, around me. Chunks of snow are bursting out the door. And small grains of snow that look like sugar. Sugar snow. A heap of sugar snow growing by the second.

Snow's piling up faster than I can scoop it away with my antifreeze bottle that's been converted into the world's finest snow scoop by yours truly.

Then out the door pops Lauren's head, and her massive shoulders and arms. There's snow stuck to her NHL cap. She's got ice crystals in the tangled mess that resembles hair. There are flakes of snow sticking in her thick eyebrows. Snow's plastered to her snowmobile jacket.

She's a living, breathing hunk of snow. She's a human snowplough. And she's pissed off big time at me.

She hurls a scoopful of snow and hits me square in the face. "Jess, would you get your ass in here and help already? Or we'll never get this sucker cleaned out."

"Nice to see you, too," I sneer back at her, and wipe the snow from my face.

♣♣♣

I have a nickname for Lauren. Lovely Lauren.

No one in our class, in our entire school, would dream of putting the words "lovely" and "Lauren" in the same sentence. That's what you call an oxymoron. Words put together that contradict each other. Like our science teacher's name — Les More. Or the guy who delivers the Free Press to our house. Phil Emptee. After we studied oxymorons in grade five I discovered the world was full of them.

Mom doesn't like it when I call Lauren "lovely" and don't mean it. She says — used to say — beauty is in the eye of the beholder.

Only thing is she doesn't know Lauren.

As I drop to my knees to follow Lovely Lauren into our *quinzhee*, something flickers between the nearby poplars. I study the trees, but there's nothing. Just tall white poplars creaking in the wind. And lots of snow.

I wonder if my eyes are playing tricks on me. Mr. Fancy told us about snow blindness. How the sun can be so bright bouncing off snow it does strange things to your eyes. Even makes you blind.

Although there's nothing, I have this eerie sensation that something, someone, is watching us.

No one else seems to notice.

All the other kids in our class are working on their *quinzhees*. More than a dozen gleaming mounds of snow are being hollowed out. Snow is being dragged and pushed and pulled and shoved from the *quinzhees.*

Some of the kids are packing snow beside their doorways to make windbreaks.

Others are using the ends of broken branches to make ventilation holes.

Another group builds a hot tub in the snow beside their *quinzhee.* They're having a nice time lounging around inside their snowy hot tub with their faces tilted toward the sun, pretending they're in some warm, exotic place, ignoring the snow and the cold and the wind.

And there's Mr. Fancy: his red scarf wrapped around his neck fifty times, leaning up against his shovel and grinning like Frosty the Snowman. Happy that everyone's working so hard, that everyone's practising his favourite boy scout motto of being prepared.

That's why we're here at Star Lake about 100 kliks east of Winnipeg. Getting prepared. When you live in the middle of Canada where the temperature can drop to forty below and blizzards whip up in an eyeblink, you need to know how to survive. According to Mr. Fancy, you just never know when you might be stranded.

I clutch the handle of my scoop and slide on my stomach into the belly of our *quinzhee,* wishing the sick feeling in my gut would disappear. Wishing I had any other partner than Lovely Lauren.

Inside the *quinzhee* it's quiet — except for the sound of Lauren scraping snow. She's lying on her back, chopping at the ceiling with her snow scoop. Buckets of snow are raining down on her. She doesn't even notice.

Without saying a word she rolls over to make room for me and continues digging along the wall by the door.

I'm surprised at how much space there already is inside our *quinzhee.* It's tight, but we both fit.

Suddenly Lauren drops her snow scoop and gasps.

Now Lovely Lauren isn't the gasping type so I take this action seriously. I gasp too. At what, I'm not sure.

I sit up and bash my head on the icy ceiling, forgetting we haven't finished that part yet.

"What's wrong?"

"Oh, God," she whispers.

I try to look over her shoulder. All I see is snow. "What is it?"

She shakes her head. "I don't believe this."

"Would you tell me already — what's going on?"

"I think I've chopped it in half," moans Lauren.

"What are you talking about?"

"Shit!"

"Shit? As in feces? Gross," I say.

"No, shit-for-brains. It's a mouse."

"Oh." This comes out of my mouth sounding like a squeak.

I have this thing about mice.

There was a mouse in our basement once. Mom said it came up from the sewer. Tyler and I watched from the back of the couch as she chased it around the rec room with the deadliest of weapons — a toilet plunger. It was the quickest rodent alive. She couldn't even get close enough to plunge it to death.

After it disappeared back down the sewer, she put a brick on the sewer lid.

Then, when I was nine, I watched this movie about an army of mice taking over the earth. Those beasts ate people for dinner. Special delicacy — human eyeballs. I couldn't fall asleep without the light on for weeks.

And every night I made sure the brick was still there. On the sewer lid.

"Is it alive?" I'm not sure why I ask Lauren this morbid question, but it seems important.

"Sort of."

"Well — either it is, or it isn't."

"Okay. It *is*, moron. There — are you happy?"

Then Lauren lifts her snow scoop in the air. I brace myself for the sound of bones crunching. If anyone can put the mouse out of its misery, Lauren can. I clench my teeth.

But Lauren doesn't slam down her scoop. What she does surprises me. It takes even more courage than killing something.

I move in closer so I can see around her.

Lauren's cradling the mangled mouse in her snow scoop. It's lying there twisted up, eyes bulging. The snow around its body is turning red. The back legs are doing a slow kind of dance.

Lauren carefully picks up the mouse with her mitt. And she sings to it. Softly, she rocks and sings to that dying mouse.

The mouse struggles, this time with its entire body. Then it's still.

By the way Lauren hangs her head I know she feels rotten.

"It's not your fault." I thump her on the shoulder. Even through the jacket I feel her solid muscles.

She sniffs a few times. "What a stupid bloody way to go. Being stabbed by a friggin' antifreeze bottle."

She places the mouse onto her scoop and sprinkles clean white snow over it. Then she crawls to the door and drops the dead mouse outside.

"Want a tissue?" I ask.

"Got one." She places her big thumb over one nostril and snorts into the snow. My stomach heaves.

Leave it to Lovely Lauren.

♣♣♣

At first when we're back working on the *quinzhee*, we don't say much.

But then we start talking.

And while I scrape and scoop snow I find myself telling Lauren about my mom leaving and how I haven't heard from her.

Lauren's a good listener. She shakes her head and scoops snow and listens the whole time.

Then she tells me some stuff. Real personal stuff. Like how her mom took off when she was a baby and her dad died last spring from cancer, and her older brothers are looking after things. And how Family Services has been trying to find her mom so they can be a family again.

There's something else. She doesn't tell me — but I know.

She has no friends.

After that I shut up. I have it a million times better than Lauren.

♣♣♣

When the walls and ceiling are cleaned off, we scrape our *quinzhee* floor down to the earth. Mr. Fancy says heat will rise from the ground and warm the inside of our *quinzhee.* I find this hard to believe. It's the same as getting heat from an ice cube. Impossible.

Then Lauren digs a hole in the snow outside our door. She places the dead mouse in the hole. Its body is already stiff as cardboard from the cold.

She whispers something down into the hole, then turns to me and says, "Your turn."

"Oh, yeah?"

Lauren nods and slaps me on the back. I almost fall over.

"Don't you know anything, Jess? It's for good luck. You gotta whisper your wishes into the hole. The mouse will be our messenger. Like an angel."

Sometimes Lauren can be downright scary. But I don't argue. It's just easier to go along with someone the size of a small car.

I bend over and tell my wish to the hole. To the dead mouse lying there.

Then Lauren fills the hole with snow, and pats it three times.

The entire time I'm trying to think of something funny to say. Nothing comes to me.

♣♣♣

When the dinner bell rings there's a stampede to the dining hall. Mike, the Camp Director, is waiting for us in the vestibule. He's standing beside the crackling wood stove in his blue shorts. He's all brown and tanned. The sides of his mouth are turned up as though he's smiling.

I'd swear Director Mike thinks he's in Florida. Either that or he's trying to make us feel foolish wearing a hundred tons of clothing. And you can tell by the way he keeps looking down at his legs that he thinks they look nice. All brown as toast. Every once in a while he gives his legs a rub. Nice lookin' legs, he's probably thinking.

Each time the door opens to let in another group of *quinzhee* builders a blast of cold air shoots into the room. And Director Mike shudders. His knees are turning red. He has goose-sized bumps racing up and down his legs.

Serves him right for showing off those nice brown legs.

We peel off our layers. There's clothing falling everywhere. Wet smelly mitts and jackets and ski pants and hats. Snowmobile suits. Snow boots and boot liners. Wool socks. Scarves and neck tubes. Soggy clothing all over the place.

And Director Mike stands there shivering and staring at us down his long cucumber nose. With all the snow we brought in and cold air and wet clothing, the temperature in the vestibule is plunging downwards.

When Lauren spots Director Mike's legs she lets out a loud whistle. Now even Director Mike's face is red. I bet he's wishing he'd worn his pants and covered up those nice legs.

Before we're allowed to eat, Director Mike asks us to sing a song, a camp song. It's about Johnny Appleseed. Only thing is it's a prayer in disguise. I know that because there's about fifty amens at the end.

Finally we can eat.

At first when we walk up to the rows of wooden tables we can't see anything because of all the steam. The air is full of steam from the food. The kids wearing glasses are fogging up. They have to stop and wipe the steam off their glasses. If they can't find a tissue, they use the end of their T-shirts. Some use their fingers to swirl away the steam, so they can see the food. Even people without glasses are having a hard time with the steam.

When the steam clears we see the food. There are bowls and bowls loaded with food. Meatballs with mushroom gravy, fried perogies, sausages, sweet corn, baby carrots, mashed potatoes with butter in small puddles on top, and cabbage rolls.

There are pitchers of milk lined up on every table.

Along the counter are twelve golden pies.

Suddenly everyone's rushing to sit down. Bowls of food are passed up and down the tables. The bowls are flying along as if everyone's playing a game of hot potato.

I take a little of everything, except the meatballs. They remind me too much of fried mice — minus the tails.

And there's so much talking and eating and noise and steam and good smells that I forget about my mom for a while.

When the last crumb of apple pie has disappeared, Mr. Fancy stands up and clears his throat. You can tell he's about to launch into a speech.

He starts telling us he's glad we're having a good time at Winter Camp. He says our *quinzhees* are possibly, no, definitely, the finest *quinzhees* he's ever seen. Even though we won't be testing them overnight he's confident we're prepared for anything. Any kind of winter emergency.

He tells us tomorrow we'll be doing orienteering, snowshoeing, and cross-country skiing. Then he reminds us it's lights out at 10:00. We groan. He tells us the evening activity — a games night — starts in one hour. We groan again. All except for Lauren.

She lets rip an enormous fart. The dining hall empties before Mr. Fancy finishes his fancy speech.

♣♣♣

It's past midnight and by the steady breathing around me I think it's safe to go. I'm not sure why, but I have to do this. Maybe just to prove I can survive.

I slip on my jacket and boots and pull my sleeping bag off the top bunk. Then I glide out the side door of the cabin.

One minute I'm creeping across the snow past the dining hall; the next minute I'm knocked over backwards, staring at the stars.

Lovely Lauren strikes again.

"Where the hell you goin', shit-for-brains?"

"To see a man about a dog."

I've stolen this line from my dad. It works to get rid of Tyler.

Lauren stands there, towering above me. She doesn't take the hint.

"Yeah," she says, "I need a little fresh air, too."

If I flatulated like she did I'd need a whole bunch of fresh air. And an oxygen tank.

But Lauren's on to me. She knows exactly where I'm headed. She's got her sleeping bag too.

Lauren bends over and picks me out of the snow as though I'm a toy doll.

As soon as we're past the dining hall, she snaps on her flashlight and I follow her through the trees. To our *quinzhee.*

All around us *quinzhees* gleam blue in the moonlight. The wind is still. It's peaceful. Just Lauren and me and all the glistening snow.

And it's absolutely freezing. My breath hangs in a frozen cloud in front of my face. My nostrils are iced together. The snow crunches under my boots.

This must be a record breaker for coldest night of the year. Fifty-five below zero, I bet.

"That old Fancy better be right about this thing keepin' us warm," Lauren says as she crawls into our *quinzhee.* "Or we're gonna be two frozen stiffs in the morning."

"Yeah," I say. And I think about Mom and how it'd serve her right if I freeze to death sleeping out here in this pile of snow. She'd be sorry for taking off.

♣♣♣

I'm so mad at Mom. Actually I'm madder than mad. I pull my elbow back 'til my fist is level with my shoulder and I let her have it. Hard. In the nose.

Only thing is the instant my knuckles connect with flesh, I wake up.

Lauren's clutching her face — blood sprays down the front of her T-shirt.

"I thought . . . I thought you were . . . " I'm waiting for her fists to pulverize me.

But she's nodding, holding on to her nose. "I know. You were thrashin' around, talkin' to yourself. It was kinda interesting 'til you decked me. Now get me a tissue or something."

I grab her flashlight and look for my jacket. All I find inside the pockets is a soggy tissue and a chocolate bar wrapper.

She takes the wrapper and squeezes the words *Oh Henry* across her nose.

I shiver. I've never hit anyone like that before. I crawl inside my sleeping bag and hand Lauren the flashlight.

As the light flickers across the ceiling I get that sensation of being watched again.

I grab Lauren's arm.

"Would you cut it out already!" she snaps.

"Shine the light over there, will ya?"

When the light hits our ventilation hole Lauren gasps — second time in one day.

Staring down through the hole is an eyeball.

"What the — "

"Shhh. Don't move."

"Get serious," she says, dropping the wrapper and flashlight. "I'm out of here."

Then she's rushing toward the door on her knees.

"Stop," I say, bossy as anything. This surprises even me. "We'll be all right."

I can't believe what I'm saying. On the inside, my heart is doing the Indy 500. But outside, I'm this brave person. Even Lauren believes it and crawls back to her sleeping bag.

I aim the flashlight at the ceiling.

The eye is gone. An empty black hole stares back at us.

We pull our sleeping bags around us tight. They feel warm as a hug.

When I turn off the light we watch the ventilation hole. Gradually, as our eyes adjust to the dark, the hole fills with stars. Pulsing white stars.

"What d'you think it was?" Lauren asks.

"An eyeball."

"I know that, shit-for-brains."

"Don't call me that."

She's silent for a minute.

"Guess you don't know what it was — hey, Jess?"

I have to admit I don't have a clue.

♣♣♣

We awake to sunlight streaming in our *quinzhee* door.

We haven't frozen to death. We survived. It's almost warm inside the *quinzhee* — if you call five below zero warm.

When we crawl outside there's a brisk wind and snow swirls around us. It's even colder than last night. Must be a windchill of 2000. Only stupid people go outside on days like this.

There's a set of animal tracks winding over our *quinzhee.* The tracks are filling up fast from the blowing snow. Lauren follows the tracks to the top. To the ventilation hole. She says they look like dog tracks.

The whole time she's up there I'm wondering if the *quinzhee* will collapse under all that weight. Then I remember good old Fancy saying a *quinzhee* is strong enough to support a polar bear. I believe it.

While Lauren's climbing down I notice the place where she buried the dead mouse has been dug up. The mouse is gone.

I kick snow over the spot quick, before Lauren sees.

As we sneak by the dining hall we see smoke from the chimney is blowing in all directions. I can't feel my nose. Or my fingers. I swear this is the coldest, windiest place on the planet.

And there's Director Mike trying to start a snowmobile — wearing so many clothes he's having a tough time bending over. Even Director Mike knows it's not good weather for shorts.

There are wonderful smells coming from the dining hall. The greasy smell of bacon or sausages. A movie plays in my head of pancakes and scrambled eggs and hot chocolate with marshmallows.

Then we notice a large dog pawing in the snow by the door. Probably the camp dog looking for handouts.

When we get closer we realize it's not a dog at all.

It's a fox. Biggest fox I've ever seen. Looks more like a small bear than a fox, except for its long black legs and thick red tail. It stops and watches as we race up the trail toward the cabins.

By the time we reach our cabin, the fox is gone.

♣♣♣

I've been home from Winter Camp for a week.

Lauren's coming over tonight.

I don't call her Lovely Lauren any more. She doesn't call me shit-for-brains.

Maybe we'll watch a movie on the big screen. If we do, we'll let Tyler join us. He's been lying on the couch all day because of his tonsillectomy.

Maybe Dad'll tell a few jokes.

We'll eat popcorn and talk. There's still something I won't tell Lauren though. How the camp fox dug up and ate her messenger of wishes.

I figure it doesn't matter anyway.

Mom's coming home tomorrow.

Turns out her kindred spirit is eighty-four years old. Mom's bringing her home to meet the family.

I think Lauren's wish came true too — at least part of it.

I can tell by her eyes.

Mouths of Madness

Ed Yatscoff

You too skinny!" said the big man, his barrel-chest deflating in disappointment.

He stood beside a beat-up, rusted old Chevy Bel-Air, eyeing me through incredibly thick glasses as if I was in a shop window wearing a price tag. The man's left shoulder sat noticeably lower than the other, matching the car's slight tilt. Deep lines etched his tanned face, centred by a nose bent to one side, just as the right car fender was slightly crumpled into a long wrinkle. One ear looked like it had been chewed on. The driver's side mirror dangled by a coat hanger wire.

The two had gone through the same grinder. Evil twins.

I looked at myself. Sure, a bit on the lean side — but not skinny. Wasn't this discrimination? If weight was a requirement I would have worn three or four sweatshirts.

My dad had set this summer job up through a friend of a friend and I had agreed to take it.

Anyhow, this white-haired old fool couldn't possibly see properly through those ridiculous black-framed glasses. They appeared to be pressed against his eyeballs, filling the entire lens.

And to think I dragged myself out of bed at dawn for this, my first day at work, only to get fired for lack of a few pounds. What a waste of some good sack time.

I shrugged. "Your car sucks . . . and you're ugly," I said, turning, positive I had blown my last hope for a summer job. He cursed. "Okay. Come. I make man from you."

I stopped in my tracks, not quite sure I'd heard properly. Was he a builder or a biologist? I turned to see him raise his wrist, moving his watch into focus.

"We late. Get in."

The car door screamed in pain as I opened it. I parked myself down amidst a conglomeration of hammers, nails, screws, string, lumber, and a million gum wrappers. Santa better bring him a toolbox for Christmas.

"I am Louis. Boss man," he said, his large hand swallowing mine in a vice-like handshake.

His eyes stayed on me, measuring my reaction. His clipped words were laced with a thick European accent. Hungarian or something, my dad had said, the only information I had on this guy, my new boss.

"You build house before, Andy?" he asked, cranking the starter.

The engine coughed and died. Louis spewed a jumble of obscenities mixed with — Hungarian? — that seemed to wither the pine cone air freshener hanging from the rear-view mirror. His big hands angrily slammed the steering wheel.

I slid closer to the door, feeling a nail dig into my butt.

"Uh, well . . . " I hoped to evade the subject as I had no experience at anything.

His goggly eyes waited for a better answer.

"I've worked as a fresh air inspector," I said, my voice cracking slightly. "See-More Do-Less Incorporated. Last summer."

He grabbed my hand, roughly feeling my palm with a gnarled thumb.

"Soft hands," he spat.

In sports that would be a compliment.

"Open hood, Andy. Push battery cable."

I opened the hood, revealing a tired six-banger crusted with black oil, goops of old grease, some mud, and hoses swelling at every ring clamp. A wiggle or two on the cable and a few cranks on the starter, and we were away, leaving a stream of blue smoke in our wake.

Louis lit up cigarette after cigarette and popped in countless pieces of gum. Aspergum. A brand I'd never heard of.

"I got sore troat, Andy. I have to have," he explained. "You *take*."

It didn't sound optional. He held out his large meathook dwarfing the pillow-shaped white candy.

I popped it in and bit down.

In a flash, my mouth and throat were terrorized by an intense sharp blaze. I sputtered and choked and grabbed the window crank. It fell off. I ejected the venom between my feet where it disappeared into the rubble and would probably start a fire.

"You will like, sometime," he said, nodding.

I'll see you in hell first. I gulped half the water in my jug. I opened the vent to get rid of the fog of cigarette smoke. A torrent of dust and maple tree seeds showered my face.

Louis, with the aid of his prescription goggles, veered the car like a pinball between the white lines and the ditch, cursing with every jerk on the wheel. In the half-hour ride to the job site he had me searching every nook and cranny of the front seat and dash for Aspergum. I'd heard of retarded squirrels misplacing nuts . . . but people?

"I alvays have some. Keep looking, Andy."

I tried not to take my eyes off the road, hoping for a bit of lead time to assume a crash position before careening into oblivion. Nevertheless, we made it safe and sound, the armrest and dash permanently imprinted with my fingerprints. We pulled off the main road into a dirt lot beside a large mound of freshly-dug earth. Rising out of a hole beside it were four cinder block walls of a new basement.

"My house, Andy. My last house. We finish, I retire."

I envisioned him hanging up his hammer and parking his motorhome outside the Aspergum factory.

"Get tools in back seat, Andy."

I got out and opened the back door. A waterfall of tools, nail boxes, saws, drills, rope, string, and Aspergum wrappers flowed out.

"Ever heard of a pickup truck?"

Louis cursed and called for more gum, frantically tapping the pockets of his blue plaid shirt.

"Get shovel," he ordered, scooping up an extension cord and a sump pump.

The flooded basement resembled a crude swimming pool after a recent two-day downpour. A Mount Fuji of grey-white gravel rose from its centre. Feeling the shovel in my hand I knew at once what I'd be doing — forever. I moaned loudly.

"You not as stupid as you look," he deadpanned.

I shook my head, wishing I could drag him in front of a mirror. He ordered me in, not the least concerned I might be leaping into an oceanic trench.

"And get *shovel*, Andy."

My implement looked exactly like a shovel: wood handle, a bit short perhaps, and a shovel-like steel end that came to a rounded point.

"That is spade for digging," he said, a grumble rising in his throat.

He grabbed it roughly from me and tossed back onto the dirt pile.

"All right! All right!" I said.

He shook his head, then asked what I did at See-More Do-Less. It had to be the oldest joke around my school. I couldn't tell if he was putting me on or just stupid.

"Well . . . I saw a lot more than I should have and . . . I, uh, did a lot less than they wanted," I replied, trying to keep a straight face.

Louis spat at my feet and thumbed toward the car. By default, I picked the right shovel — the only one left — with a flat, wide mouth.

The idea was to drain the pool and evenly spread the gravel. Louis tossed me a pair of size twenty boots and I splashed down into nearly knee-deep water.

Louis had an Aspergum attack and disappeared. Within minutes cold water seeped into the boots. I plugged in the sump pump and flicked the switch.

"YEEOOW!!!"

A jolt of current mule-kicked me through the air. I crashed on my butt against Mount Fuji. *Whoah.* Something definitely wrong here. The sump pump lay on its side nearly submerged. I sloshed over to a nearby window well and began to climb up.

"What you do, Andy?"

The old man stood over me, holding a hammer in one hand like a six-gun and a long handsaw in the other. His boot toes overhung the edge.

"I got a shock! Nearly killed me."

"No kill you, Andy. Keep you awake."

"You think I'm sleeping? Down here?" I protested from my pit, squinting against the morning sun, looking up at Louis' silhouette. I explained electricity and water and short circuits — handy bits of knowledge I learned in electric shop at school. Safety first kinda stuff.

But Louis, who no doubt used to walk to school barefoot in the dead of winter — uphill both ways — would have none of my blathering.

He kept staring down at me, appearing as big as a bear, his eyes overflowing the lenses like the goofy-goggly eyeglasses in a joke shop. I stepped back from the wall, feeling a wild intensity in that insane gaze.

He stamped a heavy workboot on the wall and unleashed a string of obscenities I never thought could come from a human mouth. Definitely nuts. Psycho. If his head started spinning around like an owl's . . .

The chorus of blue had me baffled. So far I had interpreted a short curse as an annoyance possibly caused by a missing tool, followed by an Aspergum search. A longer, louder one — greater irritation — suggested urgency and immediate rectification: possibly brought on by being *completely* out of Aspergum or the car fender grazing a highway sign.

But this blast was an absolute earthquake.

"Look," I said, hoping my educated viewpoint combined with reason and calm would prevail, "if I turn on the pump I'll be electrocuted, zapped. You know — deep-fried in all this water here. I can't do this."

No reaction. I began to climb the wall. The hammer fell from Louis' hand. It hit the top of the wall and tumbled past my ear plopping into the sea. Accidentally on purpose?

"Now look what you do, Andy!" Curse. Curse.

As if. "Hey! Excuse me for living, eh?" I shaded my eyes. His face reddened.

Louis let out a long breath like the hiss of a tire going flat. His eyes bounced behind the lenses. "You make little pile gravel and stand on, Andy." His tone softened as though he spoke to a small child.

His voice purred when he spoke my name. "Then . . . you pull switch." His arm shot back as if chambering a round in a rifle, making me blink.

Made sense. At least I'd be out of the water. He watched me scoop gravel into a small pile. I placed the pump into a depression and aimed my butt at Mount Fuji for an emergency landing.

I closed my eyes and flicked the toggle.

Nothing but the throb of the pump. When I opened my eyes Louis was gone. The sounds of his hammering carried down to me. But every time I shifted my weight the pile crumbled and I'd be back in the water. The small steady current, like a physical humming, ran from the pump up my arm, across my chest, and through my wet boots. Black spots were scarring my heart with every jolt. A death sentence.

My brainwaves altered into vivid flashes — crazy still lifes. See-More Do-Less flashed on a huge neon sign above a factory. I couldn't make out the address no matter how hard I concentrated.

I made the gravel pile higher, reducing the juice, but had to bend over so steeply my back began to ache. This pile too eventually broke down.

My shop teacher had explained that a quarter amp could kill a man under the right conditions. If not death, doing the chicken seemed an excellent possibility.

I recalled a picture in my Electricity 101 book of a cartoon man in a bathtub full of water listening to the radio beside him. The radio falls in and the room flashes with lightning bolts revealing his skeleton like an X-ray.

A picture of me.

The black heart spots crept to my brain clotting its neurons: Louis' face appeared in my mind with even bigger eyes; his decrepit car sported chrome wheels and tinted windows; he let me take it on a date.

My back racked with spasms. Any stance longer than ten seconds became an ordeal. The only way to stop the juice was to release the pump every few seconds, catching it before it tottered over. The words of Mr. Voltage echoed in my head: "Electricity can be your friend."

Louis appeared as I reached the end of my sanity.

"Take break." He slid a ladder down.

My chance to escape. But I was too rattled to make a run for it. I climbed out, drained my boots, and wrung out my socks. He offered me a baloney sandwich wrapped in wax paper. I snatched it with a trembling hand. Delicious.

"Andy, go for Aspergum." He coughed and croaked up a massive phlegm ball.

Go-pher. Aspergum gopher. Anything to keep out of the torture chamber. A corner store/Chinese café stood on the main road behind our job site. The Chinese guy behind the counter handed over the evil packet. His last one.

"You should get more of this in — lots more," I said. "We'll be out there for a while. My boss is an addict, eh?" I smiled.

"That is your boss?" He shook his narrow head. "He have foul mouth. Tell him to stop swearing."

I passed the message to Louis as he fumbled madly with the wrapper, like a desperate child on Christmas morning.

A rumbling rose in his throat like a dragon stoking its furnace before frying the peasants. A golf ball-sized gob of phlegm swirled in his mouth. He horked it out in the general direction of the store. Mr. Sensitivity.

I gathered a few scraps of lumber and fashioned a crude contraption from simple plans in my head.

"What you do, Andy?"

"Something to keep me alive." It was a simple brace for the pump with outriggers to keep it from falling.

I flicked the switch and *voilà* — no shocks. I'd live. All I had to do now was stand there. Just like See-More Do-Less Inc. Beauty.

Louis cursed — with a sing-song lilt — a good curse. If it was possible to curse in a nice way, I guess that was it.

"Andy, you smart — like new tractor." He slapped his thigh. He tossed a two-by-ten plank into the water, splashing, soaking the front of my shirt. "This work, too," he added.

Yeah, yeah, yeah. Why didn't he give it to me earlier? His clever creation had just made my sumpsteadier/shock-absorber position obsolete. Technological advancement. One small step for man; one giant step for mankind.

"Move gravel."

So much for standing around. The pool eventually drained. Gravel finally filled the uneven dirt floor. As the mountain disappeared gigantic blisters rose up on my hands — and broke.

At lunchtime I wolfed down another of his baloney sandwiches. They had some kind of sauce on them which was quite good — a secret Hungarian sauce. My own two sandwiches weren't nearly enough. After lunch Louis found a pair of gloves for me but the damage was done. My hands were nearly crippled by flaring pain.

Louis let me drive the Chevy home. He cursed as I dipsy-doodled all the way home. Nowhere near as bad as he had but still bad.

"Louis, this hunk-a-junk's steering box is probably shot and the bald tires aren't helping and the windshield is cr —"

A fearsome grumble rose in his throat. I rolled my eyes and zipped my lip. I needed both hands and one leg on the wheel to control this coffin and wouldn't be able to fend off any slime balls.

Every night at home I ate like a horse. Mom couldn't believe how much food I was packing away, said I had a hollow leg. Dad noticed my changing physique. "Wondered where those muscles were hiding." A minimum ten hours a day will do that.

Totally exhausted and sore beyond belief, I slept like a dead man. Life, if you cared to call it that, had become working and sleeping with very little in-between.

The Chinese guy said he was unable to get in any Aspergum. He didn't sound convincing. He just didn't want to accommodate Louis.

"My wife afraid of him," he stated.

His wife often puttered around in the garden out back, a stone's throw from our job site.

She only caught our attention when she leaped from the bok-choy patch and scampered away inside after Louis launched a curse into the stratosphere.

And off I'd go, searching the town for the dreaded concoction. Most storekeepers never heard of it. While on one particular mission I sauntered into a drugstore intending to check out the magazine rack and happened to be passing the cough drop section.

It must have been the beam of light from the heavens that caught my eye. And the choir. There it sat — the biggest display of Aspergum I'd ever seen. Four packets wide and two shelves high. A shrine.

And my little secret.

I needed the daily break the search provided, even though the car was getting downright dangerous. Since I wasn't even getting minimum wage, doing as little as possible had its appeal.

"You get what you get," he'd said, after I confronted him about labour laws.

If I didn't like the pay I could quit. The theme ran through my mind most days. But having a few bucks for a change was cool. One night at the dinner table I reached for the milk container, spilling it across the table.

"*&%#@**!" The curse burst from my lips like water from a fire hose.

Dad's jaw dropped. Mom's hand covered her mouth. Her fork tumbled to the floor. My young brother and sister froze, their eyes nearly popping from their sockets. The fridge motor even stopped humming. I excused myself and slunk into a nearby hole.

Between my extended Aspergum hunts and looking for Louis' continually misplaced tools, we somehow managed to get work done. He was slow and methodical, maybe because of his eyes.

One day, after working like a pack mule to get the main floor beam in place, Louis slapped me on the back, nearly separating my vertebrae.

"You strong like bull, Andy."

During our breaks or lunch, the Chinese guy's daughter would emerge from the café, coming out back to do yardwork or hang laundry on the line. I'd seen her in the café waiting on tables.

Now and then she'd offer me a smile. I'd wave to her. A sweet little china doll. Louis, not noticing our interaction, would lob a curse yonder, breaking the blissful moment. She'd hightail inside just like her mom.

One day, during lunch, she picked her way over the lumber-littered lot wearing a shiny satin-like dress tightly wrapped around her like a pretty present. She carried a small takeout container.

She smiled at me and scowled at Louis. "This is for you. I will bring more for both of you if your father stops swearing."

"I don't think so," I said, frowning.

She gave me an odd look and pulled the container back.

"No! I mean he's not my father. Come on, look at my eyes."

She did, then glanced at Louis. She laughed.

"Thanks," I said, and opened the container. Pork chunks in black bean sauce. Yippee-ki-yay! My family was strictly meat and potatoes.

"You be better looking if you cut hair, Andy," said Louis, tearing into a baloney sandwich.

"And you'd eat better if you stopped swearing."

I dumped my working-man plaid shirt and began to wear sleeveless T-shirts. I had new muscles to display and a babe to flash them at. Amazing what working like a dog does to the body. After nailing up the outside walls I realized how powerful I had become. I could hammer in four-inch nails with a short starter tap and two good drives.

My hollow leg demanded food. Louis packed extra sandwiches for me — with double globs of sauce. I was absolutely huge, getting so strong and exuberant, gaining so much confidence, I began to hide Louis' tools. We'd organize a search party and scour the job site wasting lots of time. You're getting hot, Louis . . . hotter . . . hotter . . . cold.

At times, when he really did misplace a tool, I had an urge to kick him a good one in the ass for his stupidity. I mean, he did wear a tool belt and the missing pencil was always tucked up on his good ear.

The thought of "accidentally-on-purpose" setting fire to his car crossed my mind, just so I could see how much he could crank up the curse-meter.

Every day May Luck came with food — the same whatevers-in-black bean sauce. She would sometimes stay and talk for a few minutes. I ate the delicious Chinese leftovers with gusto while Louis sat sniffing in the aroma. But I still couldn't resist his sandwiches at break time and actually looked forward to the tangy sauce. I kept telling him that she'd bring more if he'd stop swearing — at least in English.

A tall order. The rude, obscene unmentionables continued every few minutes, varying in their intensity. It reminded me of the rude unmentionables in baloney. If you are what you eat, well, that explains Louie.

Over the weekend I caught a cold: stuffed-up sinuses and a throat so tight I could barely swallow. On Monday, driving to work, Louis slipped me an Aspergum. Just held it out in his callused palm. The white-coated gum seemed to shine and drew my hand to it like a magnet. I cursed.

Against my better judgment I quickly took it and bit down.

The toxic chemicals spread in my throat like a tomato splatting against a brick wall. The powerful rush caused me to jerk the steering wheel spasmodically.

Louis' hand grabbed the dash. I thought I saw the corner of his lip curl up.

But the gum cleaned my sinuses as good as a sewer-snake reaming through a clogged pipe. Unfortunately, the effect didn't last too long. I had to have more.

I bought double my usual complement of Aspergum. The drugstore guy gave me a look as if I was buying condoms or something. I gave him a look right back. I had banged my thumb earlier and was in no mood for snide Aspergum comments.

When I returned I found May Luck heading toward our job site with another tray of food.

Louis gave me a long leer. "Andy, you smart like tractor, strong like bull, and now, you twice good-looking."

What could I say? I hoped I hadn't blushed. May Luck smiled at me. I opened the container; whatevers with black bean sauce . . . or something similar. *Again.*

"$%^##@!*&^!" Just as natural as could be, a river of filthy epithets flowed out into the atmosphere.

Her eyes shot open nearly as wide as Louis'. Her slender frame shuddered.

Before the curses had even ended I regretted losing control.

Her hand went to her mouth. "He *is your father!*" She stormed away as if she'd left a wok on the stove.

Louis slapped my back heartily, splashing black bean sauce onto my jeans. I handed him a plastic fork and together we dug into the tray, horking loogies between bites and cursing every slippery vegetable.

For dessert we slipped out the baloney centers from his sandwiches and lapped at the secret sauce. Just like Oreos.

Notes on Contributors

DIANA C. ASPIN was born in Blackpool, England and currently resides in Brampton, Ontario. Her stories have been widely published across Canada and throughout the world. She says of writing "Mom?!": "A friend of mine died and I dreamed she was East Indian. Which got me thinking about Jung and dreams and synchronicity and all the mysteries surrounding us, the questions which will never be answered, and how we deal with loss: and so, "Mom?!".

RECOMMENDED: *Bone Dance,* by Martha Brooks.

CHERYL ARCHER was born and lives in Winnipeg, Manitoba. She has written extensively in both fiction and non-fiction, and is the author of *Snow Watch* (Kids Can Press, 1994). About writing "Wishing on the Mouse" she says: "While I was helping out at my daughter's winter camp I heard a story about two girls who had slept in a *quinchee* and were very startled to discover an eye peering at them through the ventilation hole. That image haunted me until I finally wrote a story about it."

RECOMMENDED: *Uncle Ronald,* by Brian Doyle; *The Maestro,* by Tim Wynne-Jones; *The Crying Jesus,* by R.P. MacIntyre.

BEVERLEY A. BRENNA is a freelance writer and children's storyteller living in Saskatoon, Saskatchewan. She is the author of a picture book for children titled *Daddy Long Legs at Birch Lane* (Soundprints Press, 1991) and a young adult novel, *Spider Summer* (Nelson Canada, 1997). She says of her story: "Toe Jam" is based on a true experience (mine) between a vacuum and a toe and yes, the fire department was involved."

RECOMMENDED: *Laughs,* Ed. Claire Mackay.

KAREN KROSSING was born in Richmond Hill, Ontario and currently resides in Toronto. Writing has been a passion of Karen's since high school, and "Dragon's Breath" is her first published story. She says that "the inspiration for "Dragon's Breath" came in a flash, and it was a joy to write, although challenging. It is a story for anyone who can envision the power of words and where they can take us."

RECOMMENDED: *Awake and Dreaming,* by Kit Pearson.

SHELLEY A. LEEDAHL was born in Kyle, Saskatchewan and currently lives and writes in Saskatoon. She is a widely-published poet and young adult author: her publications include a collection of fiction, *Sky Kickers* (Thistledown,

1994) and a very successful collection of poetry, *A Few Words for January* (Thistledown, 1990), in addition to a children's picture book, *The Bone Talker* (Red Deer College Press, 1997), and a young adult novel, *Riding Planet Earth* (Roussan, 1997). Commenting on her story Leedahl states: "Teenage girls sometimes have adult decisions to make. Although "Obedience" is guised in humour, Kailey wrestles with a serious issue: her future.

RECOMMENDED: *The Second Season of Jonas MacPherson*, by Lesley Choyce.

R.P. MACINTYRE lives in Saskatoon, Saskatchewan and is one of Canada's most successful and acclaimed writers of young adult fiction. His previous publications include "The Rink", originally published in *The Blue Jean Collection* (Thistledown, 1992) which won the 1993 Vicky Metcalfe Short Story Award and has since been made into a feature film, *Yuletide Blues* (Thistledown, 1991), and *The Crying Jesus* (Thistledown, 1996). He is also the editor of the award-winning *Takes: Stories for Young Adults*. MacIntyre's inspiration for "The Gene Thief" is succinct: "What if Job was seventeen? And lived on the prairies?"

RECOMMENDED: *Hamlet*.

BARRY MATHIAS was born in Newbury-Berks, England and lives on North Pender Island, British Columbia. He has published his stories extensively in the United Kingdom, and has a novel to his credit, *The Power in the Dark* (Salal Press, 1997). Concerning his story "The Suitor or Three Stages in a Romance", Mathias says: "Everyone falls in love, but not everyone finds it easy! I suggest you compare the first paragraphs in each stage: they create the mood."

RECOMMENDED: *The Power in the Dark*, by Barry Mathias.

ERIC NICOL was born in Kingston, Ontario and now lives and writes in Vancouver, British Columbia. He has been publishing acclaimed work for almost fifty years, and has been awarded the Stephen Leacock Medal for Humour three times. His previous works include *Sense and Nonsense* (Ryerson Press, 1948), *Girdle Me a Globe* (Ryerson Press, 1958), *The Roving I* (Ryerson Press, 1961), and *Say, Uncle* (Harper, 1961). He says that "First Date" is "an attempt to capture the agony of first-dating. You are *not* alone."

RECOMMENDED: *Panorama*, Alberta Education, 1979.

JACQUELINE PEARCE was born in Vancouver, and currently lives in Burnaby, British Columbia. A newcomer to the Canadian literary scene, Pearce brings an innovative perspective and subtle touch to her stories for young readers. She says that "The Trickster" is "inspired by the reality and legend of Coyote, the Trickster and Transformer. This story is about the transformative power of imagination and inner resources."

RECOMMENDED: *Back of Beyond*, by Sarah Ellis.

JANICE SCOTT was born in London, Ontario and currently resides in Thornhill. An aspiring writer who brings subtlety and humour to her characters, this is Scott's first short fiction publication. Commenting on the inspiration for "I Need My Privacy", Scott notes that "much energy and worry seems to be devoted to physical appearance, particularly during adolescence. But usually sometime during this time in life there is at least one experience that makes it all too apparent that 'looks aren't everyhting'."

RECOMMENDED: *Saying Goodbye,* by Linda Holeman.

SHARON STEWART was born in Kamloops, British Columbia and resides in Toronto. Her previous publications for young adults are the novels *The Minstrel Boy* (Napoleon Publishing, 1997) and *The Dark Tower* (Scholastic Canada, 1998). According to Stewart "Flying Toasters" had simple beginnings: "I have a screensaver that makes all kinds of random sine wave patterns. It's relaxing to watch it, and that gave me the idea for the story."

RECOMMENDED: *Adam and Eve* and *Pinch Me,* by Julie Johnston.

JENNIFER TAYLOR was born in Hamilton, Ontario and now lives in Sooke, British Columbia. Her story "The Pattern of Magic" appeared in *The Blue Jean Collection* (Thistledown, 1992) and a number of her stories have been published in the fantasy magazine *Bardic Runes.* Taylor's advice to aspiring writers is sound: "The old saying Practice makes Perfect applies whether you are learning to juggle or to play a musical instrument, or to write. But don't make perfection your god or you'll never succeed. All things are difficult before they are easy."

RECOMMENDED: *Sabriel*, by Garth Nix.

ED YATSCOFF was born in Welland, Ontario and currently resides in Beaumont, Alberta. His story "Scarecrow" appeared in *Takes: Stories for Young Adults* (Thistledown, 1996), he has published a novel for young adults, *Ransom* (Northwest Publishers, 1996), and has written a collection of stories titled *Odd Jobs*. Yatscoff's take on his own story is that "weirdness, at times, can be refreshing."

RECOMMENDED: *The Pigman*, by Paul Zindel.